DANGER LIES IN WAIT
IN THE SWAMPY WILDS...

Clint did as his friend told him, squinting his eyes, and straining for a closer look, and then he saw it. The log moved, gliding through the water, and suddenly he saw the eyes and the long snout.

"Jesus," he said, "it's huge."

"You ought to see it with its mouth open."

The two men stood there and watched as the alligator slowly moved by them.

"Just watch," Bragan said. They watched for several minutes until suddenly the alligator opened its mouth and closed it, as if it was yawning.

"Jesus," Clint said, in awe, "look at the size of the mouth—and the teeth!"

During the walk back to the horses, Bragan said, "Now I'm gonna tell you something you won't believe. Some of the Seminoles? They like to wrestle with the alligators."

DON'T MISS THESE
ALL-ACTION WESTERN SERIES
FROM THE BERKLEY PUBLISHING GROUP

THE GUNSMITH by J. R. Roberts
   Clint Adams was a legend among lawmen, outlaws, and ladies. They called him . . . the Gunsmith.

LONGARM by Tabor Evans
   The popular long-running series about U.S. Deputy Marshal Long—his life, his loves, his fight for justice.

LONE STAR by Wesley Ellis
   The blazing adventures of Jessica Starbuck and the martial arts master, Ki. Over eight million copies in print.

SLOCUM by Jake Logan
   Today's longest-running action Western. John Slocum rides a deadly trail of hot blood and cold steel.

THE GUNSMITH

157

SEMINOLE VENGEANCE

J. R. ROBERTS

J

JOVE BOOKS, NEW YORK

SEMINOLE VENGEANCE

A Jove Book / published by arrangement with
the author

PRINTING HISTORY
Jove edition / January 1995

ISBN: 0-515-11530-4

A JOVE BOOK®
Jove Books are published by The Berkley Publishing Group,
200 Madison Avenue, New York, New York 10016.
JOVE and the "J" design are trademarks
belonging to Jove Publications, Inc.

PRINTED IN THE UNITED STATES OF AMERICA

10 9 8 7 6 5 4 3 2 1

THE GUNSMITH

157

SEMINOLE VENGEANCE

ONE

The blonde's name was Sherry Hastings, and she smelled like sweet lilacs. Her skin was as smooth as silk beneath Clint Adams's mouth, and her nipples reacted immediately to the touch of his tongue. He circled them first, then used the very tip of his tongue to wet them before taking them between his teeth and nibbling on them, gently at first, and then harder.

"Oooh," she moaned, holding his head in her hands, "bite them harder, Clint . . . harder! You're being too gentle!"

"I'll hurt you," he said.

She laughed and said, "A little pain never hurt anyone."

That's when he knew he was in for a helluva night.

• • •

Clint had been in Louisiana for the past two weeks. It had been some time since he'd last been in the state; his previous trips had been to New Orleans. He'd decided he wanted to see a little more of the state and had been traveling around on Duke, his big black gelding, until he found this place, a small town called St. Genevieve. Actually, the town itself was like many others, but it was here that he ran into Sherry Hastings.

Earlier that evening he had been playing in a poker game with four other men when she entered the saloon and asked if she could take the empty seat.

"Unless you gentlemen object to playing with a lady," she had added. Clint was impressed with her because she had used her tone of voice to challenge the men at the table, and they had all taken the bait.

"Please," he had said, "join us," and she took the chair directly across from him.

She was wearing a high-necked dress, a very flattering shade of dark blue, just tight enough to show how well-endowed she was. She was full-breasted, round-hipped, with a small waist and beautiful hands. If she had worn a more revealing, low-cut dress, Clint was sure she would have taken most of the men at the table out of their game. Apparently, she didn't feel the need for such tactics.

Her eyes were blue, made even more so by the dress she was wearing, and her blonde hair was piled on top of her head. He wondered how long her hair would reach if he pulled a pin from it and allowed it to tumble down. Past her waist, he was willing to bet.

For the next two hours she proceeded to win almost every hand that Clint did not, and by the end of that time they had most of the money at the table split between them. It took all the willpower he had not to let her beauty take him out of his game.

"If I didn't know better," Jim Parnell said, "I would swear you two were working together. When you don't win a hand, Adams, she does."

"It seems that way," Clint said.

Parnell was losing because he was more interested in looking at Sherry's face and breasts than he was in looking at his cards.

"Well, *I* don't know no better," Denny Collins said.

Clint had been watching Collins for the past hour. If there was going to be any trouble at the table, it was going to come from him. The other three men had been losing in silence, with an occasional epithet when they lost a particularly brutal hand, but Collins had been pissing and moaning louder and louder with each successive hand.

While Parnell was losing because he was ogling Sherry, Will Gore and Rick Eberhardt were losing because of bad luck. They had good hands; they just weren't good enough.

Denny Collins, however, was losing simply

because he was a bad player.

"What's that supposed to mean, Collins?" Clint asked. He felt that if he didn't nip this in the bud now it might erupt into violence.

Collins, a dark-haired, square-jawed man in his mid-thirties scowled at him and then looked away.

"I'm just sayin' we don't know that you and the lady ain't workin' together, that's all."

"Are you accusing Mr. Adams and myself of cheating?" Sherry Hastings asked.

Collins looked at her, then looked away. He looked at the other players, as if for support.

"Well, don't it seem strange to you that they're the only two who're winnin' since she sat down?"

"Dennis," Rick Eberhardt said, "they're good players." Eberhardt was the oldest player at the table, a sixtyish man with snow-white hair who happened to be the mayor of St. Genevieve. "Don't cause a scene, Dennis," he said.

"Are you sayin' I ain't a good player?"

Eberhardt tightened his lips.

"Mr. Eberhardt might not say it," Sherry Hastings said, "but I will. The other players at this table know what they're doing, Mr. Collins, although Mr. Parnell is rather more interested in my breasts than he is in his cards. Nevertheless, I would venture to say that everyone but you is at least a decent card player."

While Parnell blushed, Collins glared at her and said, "What are you tryin' to say?"

She smiled and said, "I wasn't *trying* to say anything, Mr. Collins. I *was* saying, and am saying, that you are a bad poker player."

"I am not!" Collins snapped. "Will, you know me. Ain't I a good player?"

Will Gore sighed and said, "Denny, there are plenty of other things you do better than play poker."

"That ain't so!" Collins turned to Clint. "Adams?"

"Me?" Clint said. "You accuse me of cheating, and then you want me to tell you that you're a good poker player? Collins, you are possibly the worst poker player I ever saw."

At that Collins stood up so quickly that his chair crashed back onto the floor. He was wearing a worn Colt on his hip, and his right hand hovered dangerously close to it.

"Take it back!"

"Or what?" Clint asked.

"Or go for your gun."

Clint just stared at the man.

"Denny," Eberhardt said, "have you gone insane? Are you going to draw on the Gunsmith because he said you were a bad poker player? Is that enough to die for?"

Collins's eyes went back and forth between Eberhardt and Clint before he dropped his hand away from his gun.

"Good move, Den," Will Gore said.

"Stand up," Collins said to Clint. "I'll whip you man-to-man."

Will Gore closed his eyes and said, "Bad move, Den."

TWO

"Collins," Clint said, "you're being ridiculous."

"Stand up."

"The only way you can prove you're not a bad poker player is to sit down and start winning."

"I can't do that if you and this bitch are cheating!" Collins snapped.

"You're being an ass," Clint said.

"Dennis, sit down," Eberhardt said.

"Stay out of this, Mayor," Collins said. "You wouldn't back me, so just butt out."

Clint watched as Sherry Hastings stood up. He hadn't noticed it before, but she was very tall as well as full-bodied, which meant that when she hit Dennis Collins on the jaw she did so with some weight behind it.

"Mr. Collins?"

When Collins turned to face her, she swung and hit him in the face with her right fist.

His head snapped back and he staggered several steps before he was able to regain his balance.

"I don't like being called a cheater," she told him coldly. "Or a bitch."

All the action in the saloon came to a halt as people stopped and stared at her in awe. Possibly they had never seen a woman haul off and slug a man before, but it was certainly what a lot of men would have done had they been called a cheater.

The most stunned of all—aside from the other men at the table—was Dennis Collins himself. He stared at Sherry Hastings and touched his fingers to his lip, which was bleeding. When he saw the blood on his hand, his face grew red and his eyes blazed.

Even as he reached for Sherry, growling, "You bitch!" Clint was moving. He reached Collins as he was drawing his right fist back to punch her and grabbed the man by the right wrist.

He spun him around to face him and said, "Don't even try hitting a woman, Collins."

"She hit me!"

"And you deserved it for what you called her."

"Let go—"

"Go home and write it off to a bad night, Denny," Clint said.

Collins pulled his wrist free of Clint's grasp and then swung his left. Clint blocked it easily and hit Collins with a right. Collins backpedaled as before, but he couldn't regain his balance as easily this time and eventually fell on his ass in the center of the room.

"Don't get up—" Clint started to say, but Collins had no intention of trying to get up. He had been embarrassed beyond endurance, and wasn't thinking clearly at all when he went for his gun.

"Don't!" Clint shouted.

Clint took three quick steps and launched a kick that caught Collins just as he was bringing his gun up. The toe of Clint's boot struck Collins's wrist, snapping the bone and sending his gun flying through the air. People scattered and the gun hit the floor and skittered away.

"Damn!" Collins cried out. "You broke my wrist."

Clint reached down and grabbed Collins by the broken wrist, squeezing until the man was almost crying from the pain.

The room was silent as Clint spoke to the fallen man.

"If your wrist is broken, you're lucky," he said. "I could have killed you easily." He squeezed the wrist even tighter, because he was angry at the man for almost forcing him to kill him. "Don't you *ever* draw a gun on me again, Collins. Next time I won't kick you, I'll kill you for sure."

Clint released the man's hand, and Collins immediately cradled his wrist in his lap.

"Get up and get out, Collins," Clint said. He reached down and helped the man to his feet. "Go and see a doctor for that wrist."

Clint pushed Collins toward the door. Unlike most western saloons this one did not have bat-wing doors, so someone stepped forward and opened the door for Dennis Collins to leave.

After Collins was gone, Clint turned to go back to his table and found himself standing face-to-face with Sherry Hastings. He'd been right, she was very tall, almost looking at him eye-to-eye.

"That was sweet."

"What do you mean?"

"Coming to my defense like that."

"The man called me a cheater."

"Several times," she said, "but you didn't even get out of your chair until he went to hit me."

"Back."

"What?"

"He went to hit you back," Clint said. "Where did you learn to hit like that?"

She laughed. "A girl has to know how to defend herself when there aren't gentlemen like you around."

"I see."

"Only I've been watching you watching me from across the table tonight."

"You have?"

"Uh-huh."

"And what have you been seeing?"

"Well . . . you haven't exactly been looking at me like a gentleman."

"Sherry," Clint said, "none of the men at the table have been looking at you like a gentle-man."

"Maybe not," she said, "but you're the only one I've been looking back at."

After that it was only a question of whose room they would go back to, his or hers.

They chose hers.

THREE

"Ouch!"

"Too hard?"

Sherry bit him on the shoulder again, leaving a red mark.

"Not if you were looking to draw blood," Clint said.

He looked down at himself and saw several red welts on his chest, which she had left there with her teeth.

"I never met a woman before who liked to bite so much," he said.

"Only when a man tastes as good as you do," she said, licking his left nipple, making him flinch because he expected her to bite him again.

"You didn't do so bad yourself, you know," she said, touching her left nipple, which had a little dried blood on it.

"Jesus," he said, touching the blood with his finger, "did I do that?"

"Mmm, you did," she said.

"Well," he said, "that's your fault too. You kept telling me to bite you harder."

"Mmm, and you did."

"Let me see the other one," Clint said. He leaned over and examined her right nipple, which seemed undamaged. He licked it and felt Sherry shiver, then he took it between his lips and sucked it.

"Bite me . . ." she said.

"Oh, not again, Sherry," Clint said, leaning back.

"Well, then, how about something else?" she asked, sliding her hand beneath the sheet to take hold of him and stroke him.

"You know," he said, lifting his hips as she continued to caress him, "I have to wonder what you like better, sex or poker."

"Sometimes I wonder myself," she said. She tossed the sheet away from him and looked down at his erection hungrily, stroking it lightly with her fingertips. "Maybe you can help me decide?"

"Maybe," he said, as she leaned over and took him into her mouth, "if I live long enough."

FOUR

Clint spent the next two days in St. Genevieve, in the company of Sherry Hastings. That meant that before they played poker they went riding, or walking, or just spent time talking, and then after the game went back to his room or her room and made love all night, trying to see who begged for mercy first.

That's what sex with Sherry seemed to be, a battle for power. She was the roughest woman he'd ever been with. That is, she liked her sex rough—sometimes too rough for his taste.

By the third day, in fact, he'd had just about enough of her aggressive sex play.

"Ow!" he said, coming awake that third morning to find Sherry nibbling at him between his legs. "Hey!"

"Too rough?" she asked, smiling up at him.

"Yes, damn it!"

He surprised her by lifting a leg over her and planting both feet on the floor.

"What's wrong?"

"It's too much, Sherry."

He got to his feet.

"What is?" She got on her knees on the bed. She looked beautiful with the light behind her, and part of him ached to get back into bed with her.

"This thing you have about pain," he said.

"Okay, I'm sorry I hurt you," she said. "Come back to bed, I won't do it again."

"It's not only you hurting me," Clint said, "you want me to hurt you, and that's not my style."

"Come on, Clint," she said, "you're the first man I've ever met who could keep up with me in bed."

"Why the pain, Sherry?" he asked.

"I need it," she said. "I've tried sex without it, and it just doesn't excite me as much."

"Well, it doesn't excite me," he said.

"It seemed to, in the beginning."

"Well, it wore thin pretty quick, Sherry."

"Well . . ." she said, looking disappointed, "I can try—"

"Sherry," Clint said, reaching for his clothes, "you're a beautiful woman, but I just don't think we're suited for each other."

"Clint—"

"It's time for me to be going, anyway," he said, pulling on his shirt.

"Going? Where?"

"Florida."

"Florida?" she asked. "What's in Florida?"

"A friend."

He pulled on his trousers and then sat down to put on his boots.

"Clint, what about the game?" she asked. "We're taking those fellas for all they're worth."

"They're going to get tired of that too, Sherry," Clint said. "No, it's time to move on. If you're smart, you'll do the same."

She lay down on her belly then, giving him a good look at her naked back and buttocks. The light from the window made her flesh look as if it were glowing.

"How about I come with you to Florida?"

Clint laughed and stood up.

"There's no poker where I'm going, Sherry," he said. "A friend of mine has a trading post in Florida, and he writes me that all he ever sees for weeks on end are Indians, Seminole Indians."

"Seminoles?" she repeated. "I never heard of them."

"Well, I doubt they play poker."

He strapped on his gun and picked up his hat.

"It's been great, Sherry."

"Memorable," she corrected. "You're going to remember me, Clint Adams."

He leaned down and kissed her shortly on the mouth.

"I sure will, Sherry," he said, heading for the door, "at least until all the welts heal."

• • •

Clint went back to his own hotel and had breakfast there before checking out. Over his steak and eggs he thought about his friend, Buddy Bragan. Bragan had gone to Florida a few years ago, taking his fifteen-year-old daughter with him after his wife, Elizabeth, died of pneumonia. He had written Clint that he wanted to go someplace new, and Florida certainly fit the bill. Unless you were talking about places like Jacksonville, or Tallahassee, or even Tampa—which had come to be known as the cigar capital—Florida was pretty much a wilderness. The Florida Keys, near the Everglades, where Bragan had finally settled and opened a trading post/general store type of business, was on the southernmost tip of Florida, and as such was even more wilderness than the rest of the state.

Clint had been feeling restless of late, which was part of the reason he had decided to take a long look at Louisiana.

Now he was thinking some Florida wilderness might be just what he needed.

FIVE

Florida was admitted to the Union as the twenty-seventh state in 1845. In 1861 it voted to secede from the Union, and in 1865 Federal troops occupied it at the end of the Civil War. When the Democrats took power in 1877, Florida was still very much a wilderness. South Florida boasted a population of only about two persons per square mile.

That started to change in 1880, and Buddy Bragan wanted to be part of the change.

Clint hadn't seen his friend Bragan in years, but then he had a lot of friends, and he had not seen many of them for some time.

In order to see Bragan he had to travel through most of Florida, from the well-populated northern region, through Tallahassee and Jacksonville, down along the east coast until he reached the lightly populated southern portion.

Part of the trip was made by means of the railroad, which had been built in 1860. Once he reached central Florida, however, the rest of the trip had to be made on horseback. The heat in the south of Florida was intense, but Clint likened it to certain parts of Texas—like San Angelo—so he and Duke were able to weather it.

He was still weary, however, when he finally reached Buddy Bragan's home, following instructions and a scrawled map that Bragan had mailed years ago to him in Labyrinth, Texas.

Clint was shocked when he saw Bragan's place. It looked as if it had been slapped together from remnants of other buildings. He sat for a while astride Duke and studied the structure, wondering if it might fall while he was watching. Suddenly, Buddy Bragan came out the front door and spotted Clint—who was shocked again. He remembered Bragan as a tall, broad-shouldered man of great strength with a full head of black hair. This man was tall and broad-shouldered, but a great paunch strained the front of his shirt, and although black hair streamed down over the man's shoulders, the top of his head was bald and gleaming.

"Clint Adams?" Bragan's voice was still deep and booming. "Is that you, boy?"

"It's me, Bragan," Clint called back. He urged Duke forward at a walk, then reined him in and dismounted.

He turned to say hello to his friend when suddenly he was trapped in a bone-crunching bear hug. He'd forgotten how big a man Bragan really was. He had lifted Clint completely off his feet and was swinging him back and forth like a child's doll. Bragan's paunch felt like a huge boulder between them, hard and unyielding.

"Put me down, Bragan, you're going to break me!"

"Ah, it's so good to see you, Clint," Bragan said, allowing Clint's feet to touch the ground again.

Clint stepped back and took a good hard look at Buddy Bragan.

"Is that really you, Bragan?"

"It's me," the man said, laughing and holding his belly. "I've put on a few pounds since the last time you saw me . . . like about forty!"

Clint peered at the man a little longer. The extra weight seemed to have settled mostly in the belly. Very little of it was in his face, which still belonged to his old friend Buddy Bragan.

"Yeah, it's you, Bragan," Clint said. He put his hand out and his friend took it. "How the hell are you?"

"How do I look?"

"Uh . . ."

"Happy, man," Bragan said, "I'm happy. Look around you."

Clint looked around and all he saw were trees

and brush and dirt and Bragan's ramshackle
building.

"It's paradise, Clint," Bragan said. "It's a goddamned paradise."

Clint looked around again and said, "It is?"

SIX

Bragan told Clint that there was a small barn behind his "castle" where he could put Duke. When Clint walked the big gelding around he saw that Bragan had a bay mare that appeared to be about ten years old. As he got closer, the animal seemed to age. He wondered how the animal was able to stand up under the weight of Buddy Bragan.

After he unsaddled Duke, rubbed him down, and found some feed for him, he turned and noticed another of the four stalls which had recently been occupied. Obviously, there was another horse in residence.

Finished with Duke, he walked around to the front and entered Bragan's store. His friend was standing behind a counter, surrounded by all kinds of merchandise, perishable and nonperishable. On the counter was a bottle of whiskey and two glasses.

"Where the hell have you been?" Bragan demanded. "I been waitin'."

"I had to take care of Duke," Clint said.

"Here, have a drink," Bragan said, pushing a shot glass of whiskey across to him. "What do you think of my place?"

Clint looked around and saw that Bragan had a haphazard way of arranging his merchandise. There were things hanging from the ceiling, things almost falling off shelves, things strewn about the floor.

"It's . . . interesting," Clint said.

"It's just the way I want it. Come on, down the hatch, Clint."

They downed their drinks and Bragan poured two more.

"Where's your daughter, Buddy?" Clint asked. "Where's . . . Holly?"

"You remembered," Bragan said. "That's pretty good, considering you haven't seen her since she was—what, fifteen?"

"I guess so—"

"She's nineteen now."

"Nineteen, already?"

"And she looks just like her mother."

Clint frowned. He had probably seen Buddy's wife all of three times and couldn't quite recall what she looked like. Knowing Bragan, though, he figured she'd have been a strong, sturdy woman. His daughter, Holly, was probably the same way.

"She must be a beauty."

"My God," Bragan said, "you don't look any older since the last time I saw you four years ago."

"Well, thanks, Buddy, but I feel a lot older—especially after the trip it took to get here."

"Yeah, I know," Bragan said, "we're a little off the beaten path here."

"A little," Clint said, "yeah. . . . Where did you say Holly was?"

"She went to a little settlement near here to deliver some items."

"On horseback?"

"Yeah, she took Lucky, a four-year-old gray gelding I bought for her a few years ago—uh, when he was a year old, that is. Actually, I didn't buy him, I traded for him, but it's all the same. Anyway, he's hers and she rides him."

"Is it safe for her to ride around alone?"

"Oh, sure it is," Bragan said. "The only trouble we've had around here are with some of the Seminoles—but they know us, and they rarely bother us."

"Do they bother other people?"

"Sometimes," Bragan said. "Some of them still won't admit that the last war—the one they call the Second Seminole War—ended in 1842."

"How many of them are there?"

"Oh, about a hundred, give or take a few."

"You got law down here?"

"Well, of course we have law down here,

Clint," Bragan said. "We're not uncivilized. We have a sheriff, and he's got deputies. Right now the Indians are driving them a little crazy, but I get along with them. They're my customers."

"Do they have money?"

"We trade," Bragan said, "like with Lucky."

Clint polished off the second whiskey.

"Another drink?" Bragan asked.

"No, that's enough," Clint said. "I could use a beer, though."

"Ah, I don't have any beer here, but after I close up we can go to the settlement. There's a saloon there."

"And a hotel?"

"You don't need a hotel," Bragan insisted. "You're gonna stay right here with us."

"Here?" Clint asked. "Do you have room?"

Bragan laughed. "It's a lot bigger than it looks."

And a lot sturdier, Clint had to admit. Even though the lumber that built it was hopelessly mismatched, Bragan had done a fine job of building.

"Come on, I'll show you. Follow me."

Clint went around the counter and followed Bragan through a doorway into a small hall.

"Here's where I sleep." Bragan proudly showed Clint a room that had barely enough space for the pallet the big man slept on—and how did that manage to hold his weight?

"Over here, this is Holly's room."

This room was bigger, but not by much. Still,

even if Holly was a sturdily built girl, she had more room than her father did.

"And back here is where you'll sleep."

He showed Clint a room that was larger than the other two put together. There were boxes and barrels stacked around, but enough space to walk between them.

"That is, if you don't mind sleeping in the storeroom," Bragan said. "We can make a bed-roll up for you."

"This'll be fine, Buddy," Clint said. "This'll do me just fine."

"Okay, then, it's settled. Good. Let's go back out front."

As they got back to the front room Clint asked, "Why does it smell so . . . so wet around here?"

"We're right on the edge of the Everglades," Bragan said. "They're mostly water, you know. Can't hardly get around without a canoe. That's how the Seminoles get around."

The only problem Clint had while riding through Florida had been the mosquitoes, and he mentioned that to Bragan now.

"What do you do about the mosquitoes?"

"Suffer them," Bragan said. "The mosquitoes own Florida."

"There's nothing you can do?" Clint asked, scratching at his neck.

"Not much," Bragan said. "Hey, you know what?"

"What?"

"I just realized we don't have to wait until I close up to go to the saloon."

"We don't? Why not?"

"Because Vicky will be here soon."

"And who is Vicky?"

"Vicky Moran," Bragan said. "She works for me, helps me around the place."

Clint looked around. It didn't look like the place had a woman's touch, and yet according to Bragan he had Holly to help, and now Vicky. Two women, and the place looked like this?

Then again, it was Bragan's place, and this was the way he liked it to look.

"So we'll wait until Vicky gets here, then we'll go get a beer. We'll go get lots of beers."

"Okay," Clint said, "we'll get lots of beers."

SEVEN

"When will this Vicky be getting here?" Clint asked.

"She'll probably come back with Holly," Bragan said. "Wait until you see those two together."

"Aha," Clint said. "Do I detect some romance in the air?"

Bragan stared at his friend for a moment without understanding. They'd had a few more drinks together while waiting for Holly or Vicky to show up and Bragan wasn't exactly thinking straight.

Clint had also noticed that in the two hours he'd been there Bragan hadn't had one customer.

"Oh, you mean between Vicky and me? Naw, naw, she's too young for me, and way too skinny."

"Skinny, huh?"

"Maybe not for you, though," Bragan said. "Yeah, you know, I been thinkin' lately that Vicky needs a man."

"Oh, yeah?"

"Yeah," Bragan said, "if I knew you was comin' I could have get her ready, you know?"

"What do you mean, get her ready?"

"You know, told her to get all spruced up."

"That's okay, Bragan." Clint was feeling the effects of the whiskey. "Hey, why don't we go outside and get some air?"

"Sure, if we can find any out there," Bragan said. "Gets kind of still this time of the afternoon."

Together they went outside, and Clint saw that Bragan was right. There wasn't a breeze to be had, although there was a hint of dampness in the air.

"What do you do around here, Bragan?" Clint asked. "When you're not working, I mean."

"Look around you, Clint," Bragan said. "There ain't a lot to do, is there?"

"That's what I mean."

Bragan nudged Clint with a big elbow, knocking him off balance.

"That's what I like about this place, Clint," the big man said. "I can relax."

"Yeah, I can see how you'd be able to."

"But when I do want to do something," Bragan continued, "I can go to the settlement."

"What's there?"

"Everything," Bragan said. "Whiskey, women, and gambling."

"Everything a man needs, huh?"

"Yeah," Bragan said, "and trouble. That's there too."

"Of course."

They were outside for about ten minutes—long enough for Clint to become food for the mosquitoes again—when they heard the sound of horses approaching.

"Sounds like them," Bragan said.

"Or Seminoles?"

"Naw," Bragan said, "they'd come on foot. This'll be the girls. Wait until you see Holly—and meet Vicky."

"I'm looking forward to it, Bragan." Clint wondered which of Bragan's women would be the most sturdy-looking.

EIGHT

Bragan walked around to the side of the building and Clint followed. Clint had come into the clearing from one path, and now two riders came from an opposite path. He was stunned. He'd been expecting Holly Bragan to look like her father and Vicky Moran to look like the kind of woman Buddy Bragan would like.

What he saw shocked him.

Holly was easy to pick out, because she was the youngest of the two. She had her father's dark hair, but she had nothing of his bone structure. In fact, sitting astride her horse, she looked to be slender and pretty, and she didn't look any older than the nineteen she was supposed to be.

The other woman appeared to be in her late twenties. She was more full-bodied, more developed than the younger girl. Her hair was red, and cut short, probably in defense of the heat. Holly's hair was long, but worn in a ponytail.

The two women rode up and dismounted.

"Hi, Dad," Holly said.

"Hello, Buddy," Vicky said.

"It's good to see you gals," Bragan said. "I want you to meet my friend, Clint Adams."

Holly's eyes widened.

"Dad! This is Clint Adams? Honest?"

"This is him, Holly."

"I haven't seen you in a long time, Holly," Clint said, "but don't tell me you don't remember me?"

Holly took a step back and studied Clint for a few moments, then said, "I guess I don't."

"Well," Vicky said, putting her hand out, "if I had met you before I'm sure I'd remember."

Clint took her hand and was impressed by the strength of her grip.

"Are you here for a visit, Mr. Adams?"

"Yes, I am—"

"An unexpected visit," Bragan said, and then looked at Clint and added, "and a welcome one. I been needin' a man to talk to, instead of these two females."

"Well, then, I guess you two are headed for the nearest saloon," Vicky said.

"You betcha," Bragan said.

"You're goin' into town, Dad?" Holly asked, and she looked worried. Clint wondered what the source of her concern was.

"I'm a big boy, Holly," Bragan said, his tone

almost scolding. "Don't be tryin' to mother me. I told you that before."

"I know, Dad, but—"

"The store is all yours—both of you."

"Maybe," Vicky said, winking at Holly, "we'll even clean it up a bit."

"You touch my stock and you'll both be fired," Bragan said. "Come on, Clint, let's saddle up."

"I hope to have a chance to talk to you a little longer, later," Clint said to Vicky. Then he added hastily for Holly's benefit, "Both of you."

"We'll be here," Vicky said.

Bragan physically pushed Clint then, steering him around behind the building to the little barn, taking both Holly's and Vicky's horses with them.

"You really don't remember him?" Vicky asked Holly.

"Oh, of course I do," the girl said.

"Then why—"

"Aren't you the one who's always tellin' me that women have to keep men guessing?" Holly asked.

Vicky gave her an amused look and said, "You're listening to me when I talk, Holly?"

The girl laughed and said, "Every word."

"What do you know about your father's friend?" Vicky asked.

"Everything," Holly said. "What do you want to know?"

"Everything."

Holly laughed again and said, "Then let's go inside and I'll fill you in. . . ."

In the small barn Clint and Bragan first unsaddled and saw to the horses the two women rode in on, then saddled their own. Clint apologized to Duke for tossing the saddle back on him so soon.

"You think he understands a word you say?" Bragan asked.

"I know he does."

"Not this one," Bragan said, patting the old mare's neck. "She's dumb as a stump."

"Probably got that way from hauling all your weight around."

"She's got a good strong back, this one," Bragan said with affection. "She's just getting on in years, is all."

"Be time for you to get a new one, pretty soon, I guess," Clint said.

"Oh, I'll have me a new one, all right," Bragan said, "and a beauty too."

"When are you expecting that?" Clint asked, mounting up.

"Oh, anytime now, Clint," Bragan said, "anytime at all."

Clint watched his friend pull his bulk up into the saddle and watched the horse for some sign that she was wavering beneath the weight. Apparently, Bragan knew his mount, for the mare didn't flinch.

"Let's go," Bragan said, "we're wastin' valuable drinkin' time."

"Tell me something, Buddy."

"What?"

"Why did Holly look so worried when you said you were goin' to the settlement?"

"That girl, she's like a mother," Bragan said. "It's probably because last time I went I got roarin' drunk. She's a worrier, Clint, just like her mother was. Let's don't let her keep us from havin' a good time, huh?"

"Okay."

"And after we're done," Bragan said, giving his friend a sly look, "you can come back and talk to Vicky some more, huh?"

NINE

When Clint and Bragan rode into the settlement, Clint saw many of the buildings had the same look as his friend's store, as if they had been built from wood that was left over or taken from other buildings. In some cases, however, structures were made of wood, canvas, and even cardboard.

"Does this settlement have a name?" Clint asked.

"Well," Bragan said, "most of the people around here call it Neverglades, but that's just their idea of a joke."

Clint saw a sign outside one structure that said: NEVERGLADES SALOON.

"It looks like some of them take it seriously enough," he observed.

Bragan saw where Clint was looking and said, "That's where we're headed, pard. Let's go."

They rode up to the front of the Neverglades Saloon, dismounted, secured their mounts, and went inside.

The bar was on the right and was made up of pieces of wood stacked on barrel heads. One section looked like an old door.

There were real tables and chairs, and Clint was sure someone had gone to some expense to bring those in. Right now most of the seven or eight tables were occupied, and he noticed that there weren't many friendly looks thrown Buddy Bragan's way. In fact, as they entered, one man very deliberately stood up and, with a disgusted look on his face, stalked out.

"What was that all about?" Clint asked.

"Not everybody likes me," Bragan said. "Hey Al!" he called to the bartender. "A beer for me and my friend."

Al, a tall, skinny man in his thirties wearing a dirty white apron, came walking over and leaned on the bar.

"I ain't supposed to serve you, Buddy."

"I don't wanna hear that, Al," Bragan said. "My money's as good as anybody's."

"That ain't what most people think—"

"Al," Bragan said, cutting the man off, "you're embarrassing me in front of my friend. Now bring me two beers before I get good and mad."

Al tried to stand up to Bragan's stare but finally looked away and said, "All right."

When he came back with the beers, he didn't

look directly at Buddy or Clint, just set them
down and walked away.

"Does this have something to do with why
Holly was nervous about you coming to town,
Buddy?"

Bragan took a healthy swallow of his beer and
looked at his friend.

"It might."

"You want to tell me about it?"

"It's just a little bit of trouble, Clint," Bragan
said. "It'll go away by itself."

"Are you sure?"

"Well, sure I'm sure."

"Why don't you tell me about it anyway,
Bragan," Clint said, "just for something to do."

The man who had left the saloon when Clint and
Bragan entered was named Greg Fellows. When
he got outside, he headed for the north end of
town, where the finest building in the settlement
stood. It was a one-story house constructed from
brand-new wood and freshly painted. He walked
up to the front door and knocked. The door was
opened by a handsome woman in her forties,
who would have looked even more handsome
if she had not appeared so harried. She had gray-
streaked hair piled up on her head, but more than
a few stray tendrils were hanging down over her
forehead.

"What is it, Greg?"

"I got to see your husband, Mrs. Wilder."

She didn't look happy about it, but she knew

better than to keep her husband's business associates standing at the front door.

"Very well," she said, stepping back, "come inside. I'll tell him you're here."

She closed the door and disappeared into the recesses of the house. Fellows stood just inside the front door, hands clasped in front of him. Instead of the woman returning to take him to her husband, James Wilder himself appeared. Unlike his wife—and as always—he seemed dapper and collected. Fellows—sweating heavily himself—wondered how the man managed to remain so unruffled even in the most oppressive of heat.

Wilder, tall, gray-haired, with the build and bearing of a man ten years his junior, stopped when he saw Greg Fellows standing just inside the door.

"What is it, Greg? I'm quite busy."

"It's Buddy Bragan, Mr. Wilder."

"What about him?"

"He's over at your saloon."

Wilder stiffened.

"Is he being served?"

"I didn't stop to take notice, sir," Fellows admitted. "When he came in, I left and came right here."

Wilder took a moment to think, biting his lower lip.

"Get some of the other boys and meet me outside the saloon in ten minutes."

"Okay, Mr. Wilder."

"And Fellows?"

"Yessir?"

"You know which boys to get, right?"

Fellows smiled. "I know which ones, Mr. Wilder."

"Then go do it."

As Fellows left, Wilder turned and went back into the house. As he entered the living room, his wife was standing there, waiting.

"I have to go out," he told her.

"Why?"

"Business."

"What kind of business?"

He glared at her and said, "*My* business, Martha."

He strapped on his gun and then lifted a lightweight white jacket from the back of a chair and slipped into it. Even Martha Wilder didn't know how her husband did it. How could he wear a jacket like that and still look cool? The heat seemed to have no effect on the man whatsoever.

"Will you be back for dinner?" she asked.

"Yes."

"I'll wait then."

"Fine."

She knew better than to ask him anything else and just watched as he walked away from her and out the front door. When she heard the door close behind him, she sank down into one of the chairs and wished to God she had the strength to leave him, and Florida, once and for all.

TEN

"Selling guns to the Seminoles?" Clint repeated. "You call that a *little* trouble?"

"I've been *accused* of selling guns to the Seminoles," Bragan said. "I do a lot of business with them Indians, and I guess that's why folks figure I'm the one sellin' them guns."

"What have they been doing with the guns?" Clint asked.

"Stirrin' up trouble. There have been some robberies, and a couple of people have been killed—"

"Killed? And you're accused of selling the guns they've been using? I don't call that a small problem, Bragan. That doesn't sound like something that will just pass."

"It'll be okay, believe me," Bragan said. "I ain't sellin' guns, Clint, and that's all there is to it."

"What about the people around here?" Clint asked. "How do they feel about it?"

"Well . . . some of them can get pretty ornery," Bragan admitted.

"Is that why Holly was worried about you coming here with me?"

"Oh, yeah, but like I said, Clint, she worries a lot. I been in a couple of scrapes since this whole thing started. . . ."

"What about the sheriff?"

"What about him?"

"What does he think?"

"Him? He couldn't find his butt with both hands."

"But it's his job to find out who *is* selling guns to the Seminoles, right?"

"Right."

"At least until the Federal government decides to get involved."

"Oh, they won't."

"Why not?"

"Because we're only talkin' about a handful of Indians, Clint. This is not Geronimo and the Apaches, you know. The Seminoles haven't had a real leader since Osceola died over forty years ago; there ain't enough of them to interest the government."

Clint started to say something when four men suddenly entered the saloon, which did not have batwing doors. The sound of the door opening caught everybody's attention, and following the four men in was a fifth man, wearing a white jacket. Clint wondered how the man managed that without sweating.

"It looks like we've got company," Clint said. It didn't take a genius to sense trouble in the air, not after what Bragan had just been telling him.

Bragan turned around just as the man in the white jacket was approaching him.

"Well, well, Wilder," Bragan said, "to what do I owe this pleasure?"

"I thought I told you never to come in here again, Bragan," Wilder said. The four men fanned out behind him.

"Wilder, let me introduce you to my friend—"

"I don't want to meet your friend, Bragan," Wilder said, "I just want you out of my saloon."

"This is my friend, Clint Adams," Bragan said, continuing as if the man hadn't spoken. "Clint, this is Mr. Wilder, and he owns this fine establishment."

"Mr. Wilder."

"Wilder, here, is one of the people who thinks I'm selling guns to the Indians," Bragan said. "In fact, I think he's the one who started the rumor."

"It's not a rumor. . . . What did you say your friend's name was?"

"Boss," one of the other men said, "you want us to throw him and his friend—"

"Adams," Bragan repeated, "Clint Adams."

Clint could see by the look in Wilder's eyes that he recognized the name. He wondered now if his friend had brought him here specifically for this reason. If he had, Bragan could be angry, but that would come later.

"Mr. Adams . . ." Wilder said. "Are you just in the area visiting?"

"That's right."

"Staying long?"

"I'm not sure."

"Boss—" the man behind him said, but Wilder silenced him with a chopping motion of his hand.

"Finish your beer, Bragan," Wilder said, "and then get out—you and your friend."

"Sure, Wilder," Bragan said. "It's time for us to get going, anyway."

The four men standing behind Wilder all looked confused. Obviously, they thought they were going to be needed to toss Bragan out of the saloon, but once Wilder realized who Clint was he had changed his plans.

"Adams," Wilder said, "you should pick your friends a little more carefully."

"I do, Wilder," Clint said. "I take great care in choosing my friends, and Bragan here has been a friend for a long time."

"Well . . . people change," Wilder said. "Ask your friend about selling guns to the Indians."

"You've got no proof, Wilder," Bragan said, "nobody does."

Wilder looked at him and said, "I don't need proof, Bragan, but lucky for you the law does."

"They'll never find it."

"I'll be back in a while, Bragan, and I don't want to find you here," Wilder said. He looked past Bragan at Clint and added, "You're welcome in my place anytime, Adams, but not with him."

Clint didn't reply.

Wilder turned to his men and said, "Let's go."

"But, boss—"

"Let's go . . . now!"

Wilder herded the four men out and pulled the door closed behind him.

"It looked like trouble there for a minute," Clint said.

"Yeah," Bragan said, "until Wilder realized who you were."

"Yeah," Clint said. "Uh, you didn't happen to set this up, did you, Bragan?"

"Me?" The big man turned and looked at him. "I ain't that smart, Clint. Besides, I didn't know you'd be here today."

"That's true."

"Finish your beer," Bragan said. "There's one more place I know of where we can get another one."

"Do you think we need another one?" Clint asked.

"Well, I don't know about you," Bragan said, "but I need another one."

Outside Greg Fellows turned and asked James Wilder, "What happened? I thought we were gonna—"

"Didn't you hear who Bragan's friend was?" Wilder asked.

"I heard, but I don't remember—"

"Don't any of you know who he is?"

The four men exchanged helpless glances, and then Fellows asked, "Who is he?"

"Clint Adams?"

Four blank faces looked back at him.

"Ever heard of the Gunsmith?" Wilder asked. "Does that name ring a dim bell?"

"The Gunsmith?" Fellows asked. "You mean—"

"That's right, that's who I mean," Wilder said. "He probably would have killed all four of you before any of you cleared leather."

"He didn't look so tough," one of the other men said.

"He didn't, huh?" Idiot, Wilder thought.

"What are you gonna do, boss?" Fellows asked.

"Something you four are incapable of," Wilder said. "I'm going to think."

ELEVEN

Bragan practically dragged Clint from the saloon to another part of "town." The whole of Neverglades was only about three blocks long, with the buildings rather spread out.

"Are there people living anywhere else around here?" Clint asked.

"Oh sure," Bragan said, "all over. Like me, they built their own houses."

"I'll tell you something, Bragan."

"What?"

"This place doesn't strike me as the paradise you seem to think it is," Clint said. He slapped his hand over a mosquito that had been dining on his neck and said, "That's a big reason."

"You sound like Holly," Bragan said.

"How does she feel about this gunrunning thing?"

"She thinks it's ridiculous," Bragan said. "If

47

anyone would know if I was selling guns, she would, and she'd have my head."

Clint felt uncomfortable because he wasn't sure whether he could believe Bragan or not. Yes, they were friends, but he had seen the man maybe twice in the past six or seven years, and on and off prior to that. What Wilder had said about people changing was right, generally speaking. What Clint had to decide for himself was whether or not Buddy Bragan had changed *that* much.

"Where are we going?"

"I got a friend in town who has a small place over at this end. He has some card games, and serves whiskey and beer."

"Is he the kind of friend who will back you up?" Clint asked.

"Sure is. I think you're gonna like him."

They reached the far end of the settlement, and Clint saw a large tent that was almost like a circus tent.

"What the hell is this?"

From inside he heard the sound of women laughing.

Bragan looked at him and smiled.

"He also has a few women."

"Oh, wait a minute, Bragan . . ."

The big man gave Clint a stern look. "Don't tell me you still got that fool rule about not payin' for a woman."

"I'm afraid I do."

"Well, I ain't got no rule, and I'm hurtin' pretty

bad for something sweet-smellin' and soft. How about you have a beer and wait for me?"

"Why don't I go back to—"

"No, if you go back, Holly's gonna ask you where I am, and if you tell 'er, she'll get upset."

"So I won't tell her."

"Clint, I gotta ask you for this favor," Bragan said. "I won't take long, I promise. I never do."

Clint stared at his friend, who was pleading like a small boy.

"Well, okay."

"He's got cold beer," Bragan said, "colder than the saloon."

"Then why didn't we come here in the first place?"

"I wasn't sure you would."

Or maybe he just wanted Wilder to meet his friend, the famous gunman, first, Clint thought.

"Let's go inside," Bragan said. "I got a little gal waitin' for me in there."

"Little?" Clint asked, remembering Bragan's preference for big, sturdy women.

"She likes me."

They went inside and were met by a man whose long hair was parted in the middle but looked as if it hadn't been washed in weeks. His clothes looked just as filthy. There were wide circles of sweat under his arms, and Clint could see previous sweat marks which indicated the shirt hadn't been washed recently. The man appeared to be in his late thirties, and he was easily the ugliest whorehouse proprietor Clint had ever seen.

"Buddy Bragan," the man said, "I guess I know who you're here to see."

"Is Jen free, Trench?"

Trench smiled, revealing yellow, stained teeth. "For you she is, my friend."

"Oh, Trench, this is my friend, Clint Adams. He came along for a cold beer."

"Just a beer?" Trench asked. "Don't he like girls?"

"He loves girls, and they like him, but he don't like to pay for them."

"Well, he ain't gettin' any free ones here," the man said firmly.

"He ain't lookin' for nothin' for free," Bragan said. "Just give him a beer and put it on my tab."

"You got it."

"He's gonna wait out here for me."

"Well, you go on back, Miss Miller is waitin' for you," Trench said.

Bragan winked at Clint and said, "I'll be back."

The inside of the big tent was partitioned off into smaller sections, each containing a bed and a girl. Bragan walked to the rear and entered the section belonging to a young woman named Jen Miller.

"You want that beer?" Trench asked.

"I think I need it."

"Come on."

He followed the man to another partitioned section which seemed to serve as a small saloon. There was a small makeshift bar and a couple of barrels that were used for tables. Trench drew a beer and set it on top of the bar.

"You gonna be around here long?"

"I don't know," Clint said. "I just came to see Bragan."

"From where?"

"Texas, by way of Louisiana."

"Traveled all that way? You must know him a long time."

"Long enough."

Trench rubbed his three-day stubble. "He tell you about his trouble?"

"He doesn't seem to think it's trouble."

"Oh, it's trouble, all right," Trench said. "Most folks around here are ready to lynch him. His business has gone way down and now the only customers he has are Indians."

"He didn't tell me that."

"He wouldn't," Trench said. "He thinks it's all a big joke."

"And what do you think?"

"Same thing I been thinkin' all along," Trench said. "He should sleep with a shotgun next to him in his bed."

Clint finished his beer, and Trench asked, "You want another one?"

"I don't know," Clint said. "How long do you think he's going to be?"

"Not long."

"What's this Jen like?"

"Young and sweet."

"Doesn't sound like Bragan's kind of girl."

Trench leaned on the bar and said, "I'll tell you a secret."

"What?"

The man looked around, even though he and Clint were alone. Still, someone could have been listening from the other side of the canvas.

Trench lowered his voice. "You got to promise you won't tell him I told you," he said.

"I promise."

"He don't do nothin' with her."

"What?"

"Bragan," Trench said, "he don't touch the girl."

"Well, what does he do, then?"

"He talks to her."

"Talks to her?"

Trench nodded. "That's it."

"How do you know?"

"She told me," Trench said. "My girls tell me everything."

"What do they talk about?"

"Now, *that* she wouldn't tell me," Trench said, looking puzzled.

"Why not?"

"She says that ain't none of my business."

Clint thought a moment, then said, "Well, if all he's going to do is talk, I guess I don't need another beer, do I?"

"I guess not."

After a few moments of silence, Trench asked, "Hey, are you the Clint Adams they call the Gunsmith?"

"That's right."

"Are you gonna help Bragan?"

"If I have to," Clint said. "I mean, I'm here, and if something comes up, I'll help him."

"Well," Trench said, "just between you and me, the best help he could get was if somebody would find out who really is selling guns to those pesky Seminoles."

"Isn't the sheriff trying to do that?"

Trench snorted. "The sheriff, that's a laugh. All he wants to do is lock Bragan up."

"Well . . . all I can do is help him if he asks me to," Clint said.

"He's proud, Adams—but I don't have to tell you that. You've known him longer than I have."

"How long have you been down here?" Clint asked.

"Five years."

"Then you know him better than I do, Trench," Clint said. "This is the first time I've seen him in about four years."

"Well, somebody's gotta help him," Trench said ominously, "or Holly's gonna find herself without a daddy."

TWELVE

When James Wilder returned to his house, he did not look happy, something Martha Wilder took immediate notice of.

"You're back sooner than I thought," she said, "and I didn't hear any shooting. Did things not go well?"

"Tend to your cooking, Martha," Wilder said sharply. "I have some thinking to do."

Martha thought she could have made a snappy remark back, but it was not beyond her husband to strike her when he was in a mood like this. So without a word she retreated to the kitchen.

Wilder took off his jacket and walked to the small room he used as a den. When he built his larger home, one that would rival any home in Charleston or Atlanta, he would have a huge library to work in, with book-lined walls and huge windows. He would have a set of French doors that would lead out to a beautiful stone patio.

One of the reasons Wilder had moved to Florida was because it was uncharted territory. He felt he could carve out a niche for himself—a *large* niche—build himself a mansion and become rich. Before he could do that, though, he needed to get rid of potential competitors, and that was how he viewed Buddy Bragan.

Bragan had been a popular man around here until the Indians suddenly began to appear with new rifles and Bragan was accused of selling the guns to them. Since that time Bragan's popularity had dropped considerably.

Now, however, the man had help, potentially dangerous help in the person of Clint Adams, the Gunsmith. Wilder had not planned on dealing with anyone of Adams's reputation and stature. Before he could continue, he was going to have to figure out a way to deal with him, as well as with Buddy Bragan.

Of course, there *was* the traditional way problems were dealt with in the West. After all, how did men like Clint Adams and Wild Bill Hickok get those big reputations in the first place? Certainly it was not always by being tougher, or faster, or by shooting straighter than their opponents. Sometimes it was simply by being smarter, and by acting first.

In other words, by shooting men in the back.

He decided to go and find Greg Fellows again. If Bragan and Adams had not yet left town, there was still time.

THIRTEEN

When Buddy Bragan reappeared, Trench moved away from Clint with a guilty look on his face. Clint decided that keeping a secret was not Trench's strong suit. If Bragan was observant at all, he would know that they were talking about him.

"Want a beer before you leave?" Trench asked.

"You want another?" Bragan asked Clint.

"Sure," Clint said. "One more won't make me fall off my horse."

Trench drew two and set them on the bar.

"I got to go see to my girls," Trench said. "I'll be back before you leave."

After Trench was gone, Bragan leaned closer to Clint and asked, "What was the little weasel tellin' you?"

"He's your friend," Clint said. "He's worried about you."

"A worrier," Bragan said, leaning back, "like my Holly."

"Maybe they're right to worry, Bragan," Clint said. "Trench was telling me how people around here feel, and about your business being in a bad way."

"Let me tell you something," Bragan said. "I can live off what I trade with the Seminoles. They don't listen to what other people say about a man. They form their own opinions of a man's worth, and then they treat him the way he should be treated—unlike my own people, who listen to gossip and believe it."

"Who do you think is spreading the rumor that you're selling guns?" Clint asked.

"That's an easy one to answer," Bragan said. "James Wilder."

"Why him?"

"Because he wants to be a big man down here," Bragan said. "He opened the saloon as soon as he came to town and forced two small operations to close down."

"Forced? Wasn't there enough business to go around?" Clint asked.

"No, I mean *forced*," Bragan said. "One of them he drove out, and the other he burned to the ground."

"Burned . . . do you have proof?"

"Of course not."

"And he doesn't have proof that you've been selling guns to the Indians."

"Which should make us even, right?"

"Right."

"Well, it don't, and that's because he came down here with some money to spread around."

"Money does talk loud," Clint agreed, nodding his head.

"You got that right," Bragan said. "But you know what? I didn't come down here to make a lot of money, I just came down here to live a simple life. I like havin' friends, Clint, but I ain't gonna die if all of a sudden I ain't got any more."

"Well, if these people are so quick to believe rumors about you, then maybe they weren't your friends to begin with."

"That's just the way I feel."

"Trench seems to believe you."

"Trench is about the only one," Bragan said. "What about you, Clint?"

"What about me?"

"Do you believe that I been sellin' guns to the Seminoles?"

Clint looked straight into his eyes and said, "I believe whatever you tell me, Bragan. If you say you're not selling guns to the Indians, then that's good enough for me."

"Well," Bragan said, lifting his mug, "then I got two good friends, and that's more than most people have got, ain't it?"

FOURTEEN

Clint and Bragan left Trench's tent and mounted their horses. As they rode away from the settlement, Bragan asked Clint a question.

"Trench tell you about me and Jenny?"

"What about her?"

The big man laughed. "It's okay, Clint. I know Jenny told Trench, and Trench probably told you. I've talked to him about you. He knows we been friends a long time."

"All he told me is that you like to talk to the girl," Clint said.

"And you don't see nothin' wrong with that?"

"No."

"That's because you ain't seen the girl," Bragan said. "A sweet thing, she is. Any man'd get hard just lookin' at her."

"Bragan—"

"No, it's okay, Clint," Bragan said. "I'm too old to be doin' anythin' but talkin' to her, anyway. Truth of the matter is, since Holly's mother died, I ain't had much interest in women. I used to use whores once in a while, but as time went on there was less and less need. Finally, though, I decided I just needed somebody I could talk to—a woman, I mean, and Holly wouldn't do."

"What about Vicky?"

"Vicky?" Bragan said. "She's more Holly's friend than mine. Naw, Vicky works for me. I can't talk to her. No, it turned out to be Jenny. Even though she's young, she's real smart and kind. She don't find it funny that all I want to do is pay to talk to her."

"She sounds nice."

"She is," Bragan said. "She's real nice."

They came to a fork in the trail, one that Clint hadn't noticed during the ride in.

"Which way?"

"Well, my place is that way," Bragan said, pointing to the right, "but I want to show you something. Let's go this way."

Bragan went ahead and Clint caught up. The trail was just wide enough for them to ride abreast.

"What's this way?"

"The Everglades."

"What's there?"

"Water," Bragan said, "insects, Seminoles . . . and alligators."

"Alligators?"

"You ever seen an alligator?"

"Once or twice back in Louisiana."

"Well, you ain't never seen no Florida gator. Come on."

"Why do you want to show me this?" Clint asked his friend.

"Because you ain't never seen gators like this before," Bragan said. "You have to see them to believe them."

"I don't know," Clint said.

"Don't worry," Bragan said, touching his rifle, "big as they are, this'll take care of 'em if they decide to come after us."

"That's encouraging."

"Let's dismount here," Bragan said, after a while.

"Why?"

"Well," he said, stepping down from the mare and taking his rifle with him, "we don't want one of them alligators goin' after our horses, do we? Especially not your horse."

"Duke can handle himself."

"Not against one of these, he can't," Bragan said. "Trust me. We'll leave the horses back here, away from the water."

Clint knew they were getting closer to the water, because the air was becoming more and more damp. Also there were new insects flying around, in addition to the mosquitoes.

"Come on," Bragan said, "follow me, and walk where I walk."

Clint stopped moving, abruptly. "Why?"

Bragan turned and said, "It'll just be safer."

"Bragan, I don't know about this—"

"Come on, come on, I ain't gonna let anything happen to you."

Reluctantly, Clint followed his friend down a small foot trail.

Clint heard a noise then and asked, "What was that?"

"A bird of some kind," Bragan said. "I ain't too sure which one. There's lots of 'em here."

The noise sounded again, almost like a scream.

"That's a bird?"

"It ain't gonna hurt you," Bragan said, smiling.

They walked a little further and then Bragan said, "Come here, look."

Clint moved up next to the big man, after being careful to walk exactly where he walked. Suddenly, he found himself on the edge of a body of water filled with overgrown foliage.

"How deep is it?"

"Deep enough," Bragan said. "The Indians travel through it by canoe. You could probably walk through it in some spots, but you got to be careful of the alligators and the water moccasins."

"Water moccasins?"

"Snakes," Bragan said, "deadly ones. Worse bite than a rattler."

"Jesus," Clint said, looking around.

"Look over there."

"Where?"

"There. See it?" Bragan said, pointing.

Squinting his eyes, Clint strained for a closer look, and then he saw it. Like a giant log, gliding through the water, and suddenly he saw the eyes and the long snout.

"Jesus," he said, "it's huge."

"You ought to see it with its mouth open."

The two men stood there and watched as the alligator slowly moved by them.

"Come on, we'll walk along the water," Bragan said. "I want you to see one on land."

"On land? Is that smart?"

"We'll be careful."

"Can they, uh, move fast on land?"

"Faster than they look," Bragan said, leading the way. "I don't think I could outrun one, but you probably could."

"Why would we have to outrun it? You said you could kill it with a rifle."

"Sure, I could," Bragan said, "but I'd rather not. They're really beautiful creatures, don't you think?"

Clint had to admit that they moved through the water very gracefully. How they moved on land, though, that was something else.

"Okay, there, look," Bragan said, "ahead of us."

Clint looked ahead of them and saw it. One of the alligators had come out of the swamp and was sitting on the bank. It seemed to be sunning itself. There were insects flying around it and even settled on it.

"Just watch," Bragan said.

They watched for several minutes until suddenly the alligator opened its mouth and closed it, as if it was yawning.

"Jesus," Clint said, in awe, "look at the size of the mouth—and the teeth!"

"I told you."

"We should probably get back," Clint suggested.

"You seen enough?"

"More than enough."

"Okay, then let's go back."

During the walk back to the horses, Bragan said, "Now I'm gonna tell you somethin' you won't believe."

"What's that?"

"Some of the Seminoles? They like to wrestle with the alligators."

After a moment Clint said, "You're right, I don't believe it."

"It's true."

"Why would they want to do that?"

"For sport, I guess," Bragan said. "They just like to do it."

"That's crazy."

"I agree with you there."

Clint was still shaking his head as they approached the horses and he saw four Indians inspecting the animals—with special attention given to Duke.

"Bragan."

"I see them," the big man said. "They're Seminoles, Clint."

"And they have rifles."

Bragan nodded and said, "Just let me do the talkin'."

"They're all yours."

FIFTEEN

The four Indians saw them coming and turned their attention away from the horses and to the men. Clint walked alongside of Bragan and stopped when he stopped. That left about ten feet between them and the Indians.

One of the Indians spoke and gestured toward Duke. It didn't take a genius to figure out what he was saying.

"He's interested in your horse, Clint," Bragan said. "Says he knows he ain't mine, and wants to know what you want to trade for him."

"I figured that," Clint said. "Tell him the horse is not available for trade."

Bragan translated, and when the Indian replied, Clint was able to guess what he was saying again.

"He wants to buy—"

"Not for sale."

Bragan hesitated, then said to Clint, "You know, it might be better if you did—"

"I am not selling or trading my horse, Bragan," Clint said firmly.

"It's just a horse—"

"Tell him."

Bragan sighed, then related Clint's message to the Seminole, who didn't look happy. He spoke again, his tone betraying anger and insinuating a threat.

"What's he sayin'?"

"He says he and his brothers could kill us and take your horse."

"What about your horse?"

Bragan laughed. "Mine is crow bait—or alligator bait. He only wants yours."

"Well, tell him if he's going to kill us he better start now, but also tell him that I will kill him first, before any of his brothers."

"I'll tell—"

"And tell him that no matter what happens, even if they kill me, I will have killed him."

"If I—"

"He'll be dead first," Clint went on, staring directly at the Indian, "and he'll never know what happens after that."

Bragan hesitated, then asked, "Are you finished?"

"Yes."

Bragan nodded and began to translate Clint's words. At first the brave's eyes flared, while the other three exchanged looks behind him.

Obviously, the spokesman was also the leader. As Bragan was winding down, the brave began to look at Clint differently, almost with an air of respect.

He asked a question.

"He wants to know if you are willin' to die to keep your horse?"

"If I have to."

"Clint, I can't—"

"Tell him."

"Okay, okay," Bragan said, and translated.

The Indian spoke, and this time it was Bragan's face that changed. He looked very puzzled.

Abruptly, the four braves turned and walked away, pausing once to wave at them before moving on.

"What happened?"

"He says he respects you because you are willin' to die to keep what is yours," Bragan said. "He said that your horse was a magnificent animal, and if it were his he would also die before he let anyone take him."

"Well . . . we got out of that one, didn't we?"

"You won them over," Bragan said, "a helluva lot faster than I ever did."

"Yeah, well, I think we ought to mount up and get out of here before they change their minds."

SIXTEEN

They rode in silence until they got back to the fork and turned onto the right path this time, which would take them back to Bragan's place.

"Tell me what's so special about this horse that you were willing to risk our lives for it."

"I didn't risk your life," Clint said, "I risked mine—and you only have to look at him to see what's special about him."

"Okay," Bragan conceded, "he's a beautiful horse, but he's still just a horse. It would have been much simpler to let them have it."

"Then I wouldn't have won their respect," Clint said. "I think it worked out better this way, don't you?"

"I don't—" Bragan began, but whatever he was going to say was lost in the sound of a shot.

Clint heard the sickening sound of a bullet hitting solid flesh, and he knew he wasn't hit.

He dove from his saddle, hit Bragan, and dragged the man from his saddle as well. They hit the ground together.

"Are you hurt?" he asked.

No answer.

"Damn it, Bragan, are you hit?"

"Yeah, yeah, I'm hit."

"Come on," Clint said, "we need some cover, Can you move?"

"I'll move."

They scrambled off the trail and into a dry gully next to it. Neither man had thought to grab his rifle. Bragan was too shocked, and Clint had been in too much of a hurry to keep Bragan from being hit again.

"Okay, how bad is it?" Clint asked.

"The bullet is in my thigh," Bragan said. "Lucky for me my thighs are like tree trunks. I expect I'll live."

Clint looked at the wound and saw that there wasn't much they could do for it at the moment.

"Did you see anything?"

"I didn't see a damned thing," Bragan replied.

"Neither did I."

"But I can tell you who's behind it."

"Who?"

"James Wilder."

"Why?"

"He wants me out of the way."

"Why would he claim you were selling guns to the Indians and then try to have you killed?"

"Who knows? Maybe the thing with the

Indians is taking too long."

Clint raised his head a bit to see if anyone would take a shot at him. No one did.

"What about the Seminoles?"

"What about them?"

"Could they have decided to try to take our horses after all?"

"No," Bragan said. "That brave we talked to was honest in his admiration for you. He wouldn't come back and do something as cowardly as this."

"Maybe not. Will you be able to ride?"

"I'll ride," Bragan said. "I been shot worse than this."

"Okay," Clint said. "It looks like this was a one shot attempt. I don't think the shooter is waiting out there for another try."

"I hope not, because we don't know where the hell he is."

"I'll get the horses and bring them back here. You stay down."

"I ain't arguin' with you."

"Keep alert, though, just in case I'm wrong."

"If you're wrong," Bragan said, "you're gonna be the one out there with your ass hangin' in the wind, so you be careful."

"I will."

Clint raised his head again and when no one shot at him he climbed up onto the trail. He was prepared to dive for cover again if there was a shot, but there were none, so he started up the trail to find Duke and Bragan's mare.

He found Duke first, standing calmly about twenty yards away. He mounted up and ran down Bragan's mare, which had run off a little further.

Riding back to pick up Bragan, he tried to recall the conversation they'd had with James Wilder in his saloon. Nothing had been said that would indicate the man would try something like this, but he could have decided on it later. Also, he sure as hell wouldn't be out here himself doing it, but probably would have sent one of his men. As it was, though, no one was in sight, and Clint made it back to Bragan without incident.

"Bragan!"

The big man stuck his head up cautiously, and when no one shot at him he pulled himself up onto the trail, dragging his injured leg.

Clint dismounted and helped Bragan get up onto his mare. Even dealing with part of Bragan's weight left him winded, and once again he wondered how the mare could take it.

"Let me look at that leg," he said, once Bragan was astride the mare.

"It's fine."

"At least let me use something as a bandage—"

"Clint, we're not that far from home. I can make it. Now come on, let's go before our friend, the shooter, decides to come back and try again."

It was good advice, and Clint finally agreed.

He mounted Duke and followed Bragan up the trail.

"Holly's gonna kill me . . ." he heard the man mutter.

Greg Fellows stopped running when he reached his horse, which he had left a good fifty yards down the trail. He slid his rifle back into the saddle scabbard, mounted up, and looked behind him to see if anyone was pursuing him. When he saw that no one was coming, he turned his horse and headed back to the settlement.

He was going to have some explaining to do to his boss. Not only had he missed Adams, but he knew that he had hit Buddy Bragan, who was not the target. In fact, Wilder had taken great pains to make Fellows understand that Bragan was not to be hurt.

Fellows spent the time it took him to get back to the settlement coming up with a valid excuse for his double mistake.

SEVENTEEN

As Clint and Bragan rode up to the store, Holly and Vicky, who must have heard them approaching, came out to meet them. Holly seemed to know immediately that something was wrong; she ran to her father's horse.

"What happened?" she asked, even before she saw the blood on her father's leg.

"Somebody tried to bushwhack us," Clint said.

"I'm all right," Bragan said to Holly, who had her hands over her mouth now.

"Let me see," Vicky said, gently pushing Holly aside. Bragan's daughter seemed to be of no use from the moment she saw her father's blood.

"Clint, can you get him inside?" Vicky asked.

"I can walk," Bragan said.

"I'll help him," Clint told her.

"Well, however you do it, get him inside and I'll patch up his leg."

"It's not bad," Bragan insisted, dismounting. As he came down with all his weight on the injured leg, it buckled and he fell.

"Daddy!" Holly cried out.

"Oh yeah, you're fine," Vicky said. She looked at Clint and said, "Get him inside."

She hurried back inside before he could reply.

Clint helped Bragan to his feet, and the man said to his daughter, "Holly, see to the horses."

"But, Dad—"

"Do what I tell you, girl!" he snapped. "See to the animals."

"Yes, sir."

Clint helped Bragan inside and set him down on a chair.

"I think I'm going to be cripple for life," Clint said, relieved to be free of his friend's weight.

Vicky came out with a basin of water and some cloths to use as a bandage.

"Cut away his pants," she told Clint.

"Hey, hey," Bragan said, "I ain't got so many pairs of pants that you can cut one up just 'cause it's got a hole in it."

"What about the blood?"

"Blood washes out," Bragan said, standing up. "I'll lower my pants."

"Have it your way, but do it now before you bleed to death."

Clint was impressed with the way Vicky had reacted to Bragan's wound, and even more so when he saw her clean it and bandage it. She was a hell of a lot more help than his own daughter was, but Clint couldn't hold that against the girl. Different people reacted to situations like this differently.

Holly came in just as Bragan was pulling his pants back up.

"Is he all right?" she asked Vicky.

"He'll be fine, Holly."

Holly looked down at the basin of water, which was now colored red with her father's blood. Her face became pale and her eyes filled with tears.

"Your father's going to need a pair of pants, Holly," Clint said to her. "Why don't you help him?"

She looked at Clint and nodded.

"Come on, Daddy," she said, and the two of them went into the back.

Clint picked up the basin of bloodied water, walked to the front door, and tossed the contents onto the ground.

"Thanks," Vicky said.

"You did a good job on his leg," Clint said.

"I've done it once or twice before," Vicky said.

"Where?"

Vicky looked away and said, "Here and there," and Clint decided not to press her on the issue.

"What happened?" she asked.

"We were on our way back and we stopped so Bragan could show me some alligators."

Vicky's eyes widened.

"That was foolish."

"I made the mistake of telling him I'd never seen a Florida gator before."

"How close did you get?"

"Well, the ones in the water weren't close, but there was one sunning himself . . . I guess about thirty feet or so."

"You're lucky it didn't come after you," Vicky said.

"Does that happen a lot?"

"When they're hungry," she said, "or startled. What happened after that?"

"We were getting ready to ride back here when there was a shot and Bragan was hit."

"There was only one shot?" she asked.

"That's right."

"Who fired it?"

"We don't know."

"You couldn't see?"

"We were too busy hitting the ground. No, we couldn't see."

She bit her lip.

"Any ideas?" Clint asked.

"What did Buddy have to say?"

"He mentioned this fella Wilder."

"He thinks Wilder tried to have him killed?"

"That's what he said."

"I doubt it."

"Why is that?"

"James is too busy trying to get people to believe that Buddy is selling guns to the Indians. Why would he try to have him killed?"

"Why not?"

"He needs someone to blame the guns on."

"Why?"

"Because I think *he's* the one selling them to the Indians."

Clint hesitated, then said, "That's an interesting theory."

"It just doesn't make sense to me that Wilder would try to have Buddy killed."

"Maybe he didn't," Clint said.

"What do you mean?"

"There's another alternative."

"Which is?"

"Maybe the gunman was after me."

EIGHTEEN

"You *what*?"

"It wasn't my fault."

James Wilder and Greg Fellows were sitting at a table in the saloon. Wilder usually spent his evenings there after dinner until he closed the place.

"What do you mean, it wasn't your fault? You pulled the trigger, didn't you?"

"Well, yes . . ."

"Then you shot him."

"But he moved."

"Who moved? Adams?"

"No, Bragan," Fellows said. "He moved right into my line of fire. I had no time to react."

"So you shot him," Wilder said, disgusted. "How badly was he hit, Fellows?"

"I—I think I got him in the thigh."

"In the thigh? Jesus, what kind of a shot was

that? If he hadn't gotten in the way what would you have done, shot Adams in the knee?" Wilder realized that the more agitated he became the louder his voice was getting. He sat back and tried to get his anger under control. "All right," he said, "tell it to me again . . . slowly."

"Why would he be after you?" Vicky asked. "Why would anyone be after you?"

He chose to ignore the second question and address himself to the first.

"Apparently, Mr. Wilder thinks I'm here to help Bragan."

"Help him what?"

"Refute the charges that he's selling guns to the Indians."

"And how does he expect you to do that?"

"By finding out who *is* selling the guns."

"Are you a detective?"

"No."

"Then how would you find out such a thing?"

"By talking to people," he said. "For instance, you just told me that Wilder himself has been selling guns to the Seminoles."

"I told you no such thing," she said. "I said I *thought* he was. That's just my opinion."

"Well, if I ask a bunch of people for their opinions, and then check out their opinions, somebody has to be right . . . right?"

"And what if most people's opinion is that Buddy is selling the guns?"

"Well, we don't believe that, do we, Vicky?"

"I can't believe this whole thing," Vicky said.

"What can't you believe?"

"I can believe that Wilder might lie to get Buddy in trouble, but trying to kill him *or* you . . . it's just insane."

"Vicky, that's the only way some people can see to solve their problems."

She stared at him a moment, then said, "It's still insane."

"I agree."

"What's insane?" Holly asked, returning from the back.

"How's your father?" Clint asked.

"He's lying down. He says it hurts."

"It'll hurt for a while," he said.

"What's insane?"

"That someone would shoot your father," Vicky said. "It's crazy."

Holly looked at both Clint and Vicky and said, "It was someone who believes these stories about him selling guns to the Indians, wasn't it?"

"We don't know that, Holly—" Clint started.

"I told him not to go to town, I told him," she went on, without listening. "Now we'll have to leave here."

"Leave?" Vicky asked. "Why?"

"Why?" Holly repeated. "Everyone here thinks my father is selling guns to the Indians. First we lost customers, and money, and now he almost lost his life. We have to get out of here."

"Holly, your father's friend is going to prove that he's not selling guns to anyone."

The girl looked at Clint. "You are?"

"I'm going to help your father," Clint said, tossing Vicky a dirty look at the same time, "if he wants me to."

"You can help by telling him he has to leave here," Holly said.

"I can't tell him that, Holly," Clint said. "He's got to decide that on his own."

"He's got to agree," she said, almost desperately, "he's got to leave, or he'll get killed."

"Holly—" Clint started, but she brushed past both of them and ran outside.

"She's upset," Vicky said. "I'll talk to her."

Clint watched Vicky go out the door after Holly and frowned. He found Holly's behavior strange. Surely she knew the potential problems before today. Granted her father had just been shot, but he still found her actions a little . . . extreme.

He went into the back to see if Bragan was awake.

NINETEEN

"I'm not asleep," Bragan called out as Clint stuck his head in the door.

"How do you feel?" Clint asked, entering the room.

"I'm fine," Bragan said. "I'm only lyin' down here because Holly insisted."

"Tell me something," Clint said. "How much of what she insists on will you do?"

"What do you mean?"

"Well, if she insisted that the two of you leave here, would you?"

"Leave here?"

"Leave Florida," Clint said. "What would you do, Bragan?"

"This is my home, Clint," Bragan said, "and I ain't leavin' just because some son of a bitch started a rumor that I'm sellin' guns to the Indians."

"How about because your daughter is afraid you're going to get killed?"

Bragan stared at Clint for a few moments before replying.

"Did she put you up to this?"

"Bragan—"

"Did she tell you to say this to me?"

"Bragan—"

"That I should leave? Because if she did, forget it—"

"Buddy!"

Bragan stopped talking abruptly.

"I'm not telling you that you have to leave," Clint said. "I can't tell you that. That's up to you to decide. I was just asking you what if . . ."

"Well, if she asks me to leave I'm gonna say no," Bragan said. "That's what if."

"Have you thought about what she'd do?"

Bragan frowned. "What do you mean?"

"If you say no," Clint said, "she might decide to leave on her own."

Bragan looked dubious, then shocked. "Naw, she wouldn't do that."

"Why not?"

"She's too young."

"She's nineteen."

"Yeah, but . . . she ain't never been on her own."

"How old were you when you went out on your own?" Clint asked.

"That's different."

"Why?"

"Because I was a boy . . . a man, and she's a girl, that's why."

"She's a woman, Bragan," Clint said. "Take a good look at her when she comes back in here. She's a woman."

"She's still my daughter."

"Okay," Clint said, "what happens between you and her is not my business. Tell me what you want me to do."

"Why should you do anything?"

"Because you're my friend, and you're in trouble."

"I still don't understand—"

"Let me explain something to you," Clint said. "I have a lot of experience at this."

"At what? Selling guns? Finding out who *is* selling guns—"

"No," Clint said, cutting him off, "I have a knack for walking into the lives of my friends just when they're having trouble. It happens all the time."

"Well," Bragan said, "then what I suggest you do is leave."

"Leave?"

Bragan nodded. "Why should you get involved in this? It ain't your fight."

"Bragan," Clint said, "whatever the reason, I'm here now and you're in trouble. Let me help."

"There's only one way you can help me, Clint."

"And what's that?"

"Since I know I'm not selling guns to the Indians," Bragan said, "that means somebody else is. All you have to do is find out who."

TWENTY

Clint went to the front door and looked out at Vicky and Holly talking earnestly. He stood there awhile watching them, and then Vicky turned her head and spotted him there. She did an odd thing, then. She turned her back, as if she were afraid that he was going to be able to read her lips. Holly did the same thing, and the two women continued to talk.

He stepped outside, intending to approach them, but then thought better of it. If they didn't want him to know what they were talking about, that was their business. Instead he walked around behind the store to the small barn to take a look at Duke.

The big horse was sweating, and Clint couldn't blame him for that. Still, it was probably more from the ride than from the heat. The big gelding really didn't appear bothered by anything, until Clint looked at his tail. He was swishing it in double time, trying to swat away the mosquitoes.

"You too, huh, big fella?"

Clint picked up a brush and rubbed the horse down properly. Holly had obviously been in too much of a hurry to do much more than unsaddle him.

When he finished with Duke he did the same for the mare, and then fed both horses. By the time he was done he saw Vicky coming around the house toward him.

"Hi," she said.

"Hi."

"I talked to Holly."

"I saw."

She didn't comment on that.

"She calmed down some, but I think she's still intent on asking Buddy to leave."

"What happens to you if they leave?"

She shrugged.

"Maybe Bragan would let you buy this place."

"That's a laugh," she said. "I don't have any money, not even enough to buy a dump like this."

"A dump?"

"What would you call it?"

"Bragan calls it paradise."

She laughed derisively. "To him, maybe. All I want to do is get away from here, and out of Florida."

"Where do you want to go?"

"Someplace that has seasons."

"Seasons?"

"The weather doesn't change much down here, Clint," she said. "One of the things I miss is the changing of the seasons."

"You miss it? I guess that means you weren't born here?"

"Hell, no," she said, "I was born in Georgia, which isn't much better."

"What brought you down here?"

"What else? A man."

"And what happened to him?"

"He got killed."

"I'm sorry," he said. "How did it happen?"

"He got too close to an alligator."

Clint shuddered, thinking about the jaws of an alligator and what they could do to a man.

"That's why I thought it was stupid of Buddy to try to get you a close look at one."

"I can understand you feeling that way."

They stood in silence for a few moments, and then she said, "Well, I better get going. There's not much for me to do here."

"You live at the settlement?"

"Yeah, I live there."

"Neverglades, huh?" Clint said.

She laughed. "He told you about that, huh?"

Clint nodded. "Yes, some people call it that."

"Not you?"

"I'd hate to tell you what I call it."

"When are you leaving?"

"Now. If you let me get to my horse so I can saddle her."

"I'll do better than that," he said. "I'll saddle her for you."

"Well," she said, "a gentleman. That's rare down here. I'd hate to tell you how rare."

They continued to talk while he saddled her animal.

"Where do you spend most of your time?" she asked.

"I travel a lot," he said, "but I guess I spend most of my time in Texas."

"I've never been to Texas," she said. "Hell, I've never been anywhere."

Clint didn't know what to say to that. Usually, a woman who talked about leaving where she was, in that tone of voice, was looking for a man to take her away—and he wasn't about to volunteer for the job. Not yet, anyway, not when he hardly knew her.

"There you go," he said, walking the horse out, "all set."

"Thanks."

He helped her mount up by letting her step on his laced fingers.

"You know, I don't know what they're going to do about dinner here. I'm going to eat when I get back to the settlement. You're welcome to join me."

"It's a tempting offer," he said, "and I'd take you up on it if Duke—my horse—hadn't already made the trip once today. Besides, I think I should stay around here for a while."

"I understand," she said. "The man who shot Buddy might come back."

"It's possible."

She nodded.

"Would you say good-bye to Holly and Buddy for me?" she asked.

"Sure."

"Tell them I'll see them tomorrow."

"Okay."

"And I'll see you tomorrow too."

"Right."

"Maybe we can talk for a while again."

"That would be my pleasure, Vicky."

There was a moment's hesitation, and then she said, "Well, good-bye."

"Bye."

She turned her horse, and he watched her ride off until she was out of sight. He walked back to the store, wondering if there was a lot more going on here than he knew about.

TWENTY-ONE

When Clint walked back into the store, Holly was standing behind the counter, looking unhappy.

"Vicky left," he said.

"I know."

"I guess without her here and your father laid up you better close the store, huh?"

"That's a laugh," she said. "Close the store. We haven't had a paying customer in a month."

"How have you been getting along, then?"

"Trading," she said, "with the Seminoles. They're the only ones who've been decent to us."

"You know," Clint said, approaching the counter, "that might be part of your problem."

"What is?"

"The fact that you're friendly with the Seminoles," he explained.

"I'm not friendly with them," she said. "Dad does business with them. If it wasn't for the trading we do with them—"

She stopped short.

"What is it?"

"I just thought of something," she said. "If it wasn't for the trading with them, we'd probably have left here a long time ago."

"I don't think your dad wants to leave, Holly."

"He wouldn't have any choice," she said, warming to the idea. "If we weren't doin' any business at all, he'd have to leave."

"So what are you saying?"

"I'm sayin' that the Seminoles are makin' our life hard in more ways than one."

She turned around and took a rifle from the wall, where it was resting on some nails.

"What are you doing?"

"I'm gonna load this."

"Why?"

"Because if any Seminoles come to do any trading with us," she said, "I'm gonna shoot 'em. Where'd he put those shells?"

"Holly, wait," Clint said. He moved around behind the counter and took the rifle from her.

"Give it back!"

"Quiet," he said, "you'll wake your father. I'm not going to give you back this rifle."

"Why not?"

"Because the last thing you want to do is start a private war with the Seminoles. If you kill one of them, they might come and burn this place to the ground."

"Good."

"With you and your pa in it."

She didn't have an answer to that. "So what am I supposed to do?"

"Talk to your pa, Holly," he said. "That's all you can do."

"I'll talk to him later," she said, "when he's feeling better."

"I'm putting this back on the wall," he said, returning the rifle to its rightful place. "Don't take it down again, all right?"

"Oh, I don't even know how to load the damn thing," she muttered. "I probably would have shot myself in the foot with it."

"Then if there's any shooting to be done around here, let me do it."

"Are you gonna stay awhile?"

"At least until your pa's wound heals, and until I can find out what's going on around here."

"Are you gonna find out who's really sellin' guns to the Indians?"

"I don't know if I can do that," Clint said. "Maybe I can prove that your father's not doing it, though."

"How?"

"I don't know . . . yet."

"I'd better lock the front door," she said, "just in case some of them Seminoles do show up."

"We ran into some of them on our way back from town," he told her.

"You did?" She turned and asked, "What happened?"

"Go ahead and lock up and I'll tell you."

He explained to her about the four Seminoles, and that one of them wanted his horse.

"You stood up to them?"

"Well, I wasn't about to lose my horse."

"Weren't they mad?"

"No," he said, and explained how in standing up to them he had won their respect.

"Your father didn't seem to know these particular Seminoles," he added, "but I have to assume that the ones who do know him respect him, too, otherwise they wouldn't be doing business with him."

She locked the doors and turned to face him.

"They respect him because he treats them the same as he treats everyone else," she said. "Maybe if he didn't, we wouldn't be in this mess."

"You can't blame your father for that, Holly."

"Then tell me who I can blame."

This time it was Clint who didn't have an answer.

"Never mind," she said. "I better get something cookin' for dinner. He's gonna be hungry when he wakes up. Are you hungry?"

"I will be."

"I'll make dinner," she said.

"Where?" Clint asked. He didn't see a kitchen.

"Come with me," she said, and went into the back.

TWENTY-TWO

He followed her down the hall, past the room where Bragan was now sleeping. She led him to a back door and out. From where they were he could see the small barn, but from the barn he had not been able to see the small, rock-encircled area where Bragan had prepared a spot for a permanent camp fire.

"You start the fire," she said. "I'll go get the makings for dinner, and the pots."

Clint looked around and found a pile of wood pieces and tree branches on one side of the house. He used those to build a fire. When Holly returned she had a large pot and some vegetables.

"I'm gonna make a stew," she said.

She set up a wooden tripod her father had probably made and then suspended the large pot from it. She filled it with water and left it to boil.

After that she sat down and started peeling and cutting vegetables.

"A meatless stew?" he asked.

"Unless you want to go out and shoot an alligator," she said.

"Do they eat alligator?"

"Yes."

"Have you?"

"Yes."

"What's it taste like?"

"A little like chicken."

"Is there anything else around here that I could go out and hunt for?"

"No," she said. "We're too close to the Everglades for any decent game—that is, unless you want to catch a water moccasin."

"I don't think so."

Clint had eaten rattlesnake before and hadn't found it bad, but the thought of eating a water moccasin did not appeal to him at all.

He sat down across from Holly and watched as she sliced the vegetables.

"Holly, can I ask you something?"

"Sure, why not?"

"If your father decides to stay here, what will you do?"

"I'll leave without him."

"Just like that?"

She answered without looking at him. "It's not just like that, Clint," she said. "I've thought about it for a long time. I've decided that I'm not going to stay here much longer."

"When will you leave, then?"

"I'll stay until he's out of trouble," she said, "and then I'll go."

"How?"

"I'll saddle my horse and go."

"With what supplies? Where will you go?"

"I'll take some supplies with me. As far as where I'll go, I'll go north."

"Holly, you've never traveled on your own."

"Maybe I won't have to."

"What do you mean by that?"

"I mean there are plenty of men who'd take me along to cook and clean for them in exchange."

"That isn't all they'd want in exchange, you know," he warned her.

"Not necessarily."

"You're a very pretty girl, Holly."

She looked at him this time. "Then take me with you when you leave."

He was taken aback by the request, although he didn't know why. He'd half expected Vicky to ask it, so why was he surprised when Holly did?

"I couldn't do that, Holly."

"Why not? Because you're my father's friend?"

"Well, that's one reason—"

"Do you think he'd rather see me travel alone or with you?"

"I think he'd rather see you not traveling at all," Clint said.

"You'd be doing him a favor by takin' me with you, Clint," she went on. "At least then he'd know that I'd be safe."

"Holly—"

"I'll cook and clean for you . . . and do anything else you want."

"Holly . . . you don't have to make an offer like that."

"Why not?" she asked. "You said yourself I'm pretty. Don't you want me?"

"Holly."

She laughed then and said, "All right, forget about sex. How about the cookin' and cleanin'?"

"Holly—"

"In a little while you'll see what a good cook I am," she said, "but don't judge me by the way this place looks. It looks like this because my father wants it to. He won't let me clean it."

"Holly, I can't take you with me when I leave," Clint said. "I'm sorry."

"Well . . . I've got other options."

"Like what?"

"Not what," she said, "who."

"All right, who?"

"Vicky."

"Vicky?"

Holly nodded.

"She wants to leave too," she said. "It would benefit both of us if we traveled together."

Clint had to admit that the two women traveling together was better than one of them traveling alone.

"Before you do that," he said, "you'd better learn to shoot."

She paused in her cutting and said, "You're right about that."

She finished slicing, picked up the vegetables, and dropped them into the pot. Then she turned and looked down at him.

"Will you teach me to shoot?"

"So you can leave? Your father would kill me."

"Whether I leave or stay I should know how to shoot, don't you agree?"

"Well, yes—"

"Fine," she said, wiping her hands on her pants, "teach me to shoot and never mind why."

He studied her for a few moments. If trouble came within the next few days, it would help if she knew how to fire a rifle.

"All right," he said, standing up, "get a rifle and I'll teach you how to use it."

TWENTY-THREE

She went inside and came out with the same rifle she'd taken off the wall earlier.

"I couldn't find the bullets."

"You won't need any."

"What? No bullets? What good is a rifle without bullets?"

"For what we're going to do today you won't need any," he said, taking the rifle from her.

First he showed her how to load the weapon, which he was able to do without bullets. After that he showed her how to hold it, how to aim it, and how to fire it. When that was done he drilled her, making her go through the motions of loading, aiming, and firing.

By the time the smell of the vegetable stew was filling the air, she was fairly good at it.

"That's enough for one day."

"When do we use bullets?"

"Sometime when your father is not sleeping," he said, taking the rifle and putting it aside. "Tomorrow I'll show you how to clean the weapon after you've fired it."

"Cleaning again," she said, shaking her head. "Women just can't get away from that, can they?"

"Man or woman," he said, "if you don't keep your weapon clean, it will turn on you."

"How does it do that?"

"By jamming just when you need it," Clint said. "It happens a lot. I've known men to be killed because, as fast and as accurate as they were, they didn't know enough to keep their weapons clean."

"I'm gonna go inside and check on Dad," she said. "If he's awake, I'll bring him some stew."

"I'll wait for you here."

She went inside and was back in seconds.

"He's fast asleep," she said. "We'll eat without him."

She got a wooden bowl and filled it, then gave it to Clint with a large wooden spoon.

"We made our own utensils," she said, filling a bowl for herself. "What I wouldn't give to eat with a real spoon or fork, just once."

"Surely you have before."

"Yes, but not for a very long time," she said. She grew pensive then and said, "The last time I did, my mother was still alive."

Clint didn't know what to say to that so he just ate. The food was bland, but he had to admit that Holly had done well, given what she had to work with.

"How's the food?"

"It's great."

"I'd do better on the trail somewhere with some real game to work with," she said. "You should see what I can do with a rabbit, or even a possum."

"I believe it, Holly."

"But you still won't take me with you?"

"I'm sorry. . . ."

She fell silent then and they finished their meal that way. She didn't speak again until she collected his bowl and spoon from him.

She set the wooden utensils aside and then turned quickly as Clint was standing up. She caught him off balance, put her arms around his neck, and kissed him, thrusting her tongue inside his mouth. He was so surprised that for a moment he didn't react at all, and then when he did, it was the wrong reaction. She was so young and sweet, and she was rubbing her body up against his. His first reaction was to put his arms around her and kiss her back, but after a few moments he realized what he was doing, pried her arms from his neck, and pushed her away.

"You want me," she said breathlessly. "I can feel it. You do."

"Holly," he said, "a man would have to be a fool not to want you, but that's not going to happen again. Do you hear me?"

She looked down at her feet, like a chastised child, and said, "Yes, I understand, but let me ask you one more thing, Clint."

"All right," he said, "ask."

"Would you take me with you," she said, "if my father asked you to?"

"Somehow," he said, "this sounds like a trick question."

"It's not," she said. "Would you?"

"Why would he do that?"

"Suppose I convinced him it was best for me to leave, and he asked you to take me with you. What would you do?"

He still thought it was a trick question, but in spite of that there was only one way he could see to answer it.

"Well," he said, choosing his words carefully, "if your pa asked me to take you with me I'd have to . . . take the request under consideration."

"That's nonsense," she said. "Yes or no . . . would you?"

"If I have to answer yes or no," he said, "I guess the answer would have to be . . . yes."

"Yes!" she said, clapping her hands together. "You just sit yourself down and I'll make some coffee."

TWENTY-FOUR

Holly made a pot of coffee and left Clint with a cup while she went in and checked on her father again. Clint was surprised when Buddy Bragan came out the door without Holly.

"Goddamned girl thinks I'm an invalid," Bragan said, limping to where Clint was sitting.

Holly came out a moment later, fuming.

"Will you tell him he should be in bed?"

"Would you tell her I'm hungry?" Bragan said.

"Would you tell him I'd bring his food to him in bed if he'd stay there?"

"Will you tell her—"

"Hey, hold it," Clint said to both of them. "How about talking to each other and leaving me out of it?"

"Never mind," Holly said. "I'll get you something to eat, Dad. You need your strength."

She brought her father a bowl of stew and a spoon. "Eat that and then you're going back to bed."

She turned and went inside.

"I didn't ask you," Bragan said to Clint, trying to ignore his daughter's last words, "how long will you be staying?"

"Well, I've only been here a day and already you've shown me a real interesting time."

"Yeah, it has been interestin', ain't it?" Bragan said, laughing. "Just like the old days."

Clint didn't bother telling Bragan that he didn't remember what the old days were like—not with them anyway.

"So, how long?" Bragan asked.

"Long enough to help you."

"That might be a long time."

"Who would I talk to about the guns, Bragan?"

"How would I know?" Bragan answered. "Go and talk to James Wilder—about the guns, about the shooting, about everything."

"Good idea," Clint said.

He got up and poured himself another cup of coffee, even though it was too weak.

"Who else?" he asked, sitting back down next to the big man.

"The sheriff."

"What's his name?"

"Didn't I tell you?"

"No."

"It's Collins, Mike Collins."

"Where do I find him?"

"Try Neverglades tomorrow," Bragan said. "He's usually there in the middle of the week."

"Any other suggestions?"

"Yeah," Bragan said, "your new friend."

"What new friend?"

"The Seminole who wanted your horse."

"I don't even know his name."

"I didn't tell you?"

"No, Bragan, you didn't tell me."

"He's called Otani."

"What's that mean?"

"I don't know," Bragan said. "I guess that's somethin' else you'll have to ask him, after you ask him about the guns."

"And how do I find him?"

Bragan rubbed his jaw.

"There's a tame Seminole in Neverglades," he said finally. "Ask Trench, he'll take you to him."

"What's his name?"

"Little Hard Head."

"What?"

"They call him Little Hard Head."

"Why do they call him that?"

"Because he was shot in the head once and lived," Bragan explained. "You'll see the scar."

"Okay," Clint said, "I'll do all that tomorrow."

They sat in silence for a while, and when Bragan finished eating Clint got him a cup of coffee.

"That girl makes the worst coffee," Bragan said.

"Another handful and it would be just right."

"Clint?"

"Yeah?"

"I appreciate your help."

"Forget it."

"No, that's not all I wanted to say," Bragan said. "I don't want you stayin' here until I'm out of trouble. That's askin' too much."

"Maybe I can wrap this up in one day."

"Until my leg is well enough for me to get around," Bragan said. "That's as long as I want you to stay. Okay?"

"Bragan—"

"I insist, Clint," Bragan said, cutting him off. "Okay?"

Clint hesitated, then said, "Okay, Bragan, until you're healed."

"No," Bragan said, "just until I can get myself around again."

"And then what will you do?"

"I'll get myself out of trouble."

"And what about Holly?"

"What about her?"

"If somebody takes another shot at you, Bragan, she could be in the line of fire."

Bragan looked confused for a moment, and then helpless. "Well, what am I supposed to do, then?"

"Don't put any limitations on me," Clint said.

"Let me see what I can find out, and then we'll go from there."

"I thought of something else while I was lying down," Bragan said.

"What's that?"

"What if you were the target?" he said. "I mean, you got a rep, maybe somebody noticed—ah, that's crazy."

"Why?"

"What a coincidence that would be, huh? Somebody who recognized you down here?"

"I thought of that already, Bragan," Clint said, "about me being the target instead of you, I mean."

"Yeah, but who'd take a shot at you?"

"Well, maybe Wilder," Clint said. "Maybe he doesn't want you dead, but he wants me out of the way so I can't help you."

"If that's true," Bragan said, "then you'd be walking right into his arms tomorrow."

"No, I won't. If he had somebody try to bushwhack me on the trail, he's not going to try anything right there in front of everybody. I'll be fine."

"And what am I supposed to do while you're tryin' to solve my problem?"

"Just sit still," Clint said, "listen to Holly, and heal."

TWENTY-FIVE

In the middle of the night Clint heard someone entering the storeroom where he was sleeping. He turned quickly and saw a figure standing over him.

"Who—"

"Shhh," she said. "It's me, Holly."

"Holly? What's wrong?"

"Nothing," she whispered.

She leaned over, pulled his blanket aside, and lay down next to him. The heat from her body was intense, and as she pressed herself against him he suddenly became aware that she was naked.

"Jesus, Holly, you're naked."

"I'm glad you noticed," she said, with her mouth on his neck.

"Holly—"

"Shhh," she said, sliding her hand down over him.

It was so hot that he had decided to sleep naked. Her hand easily found his penis, which was already hard and pulsating.

"Ah," she said, "I see you do want me. I knew you were lying this afternoon."

"I didn't lie this afternoon," he said. "I didn't say I didn't want you, I said . . . hey—"

She had slid her hands down even further and scraped his testicles with her nails.

"Quiet," she said, "you're gonna wake Dad."

"If he wakes up and finds us like this," Clint said, "he'll kill me. Holly, you're only nineteen."

"I'll be twenty in five months."

"Twenty is still too . . . uh . . . young. . . ."

"I'm not a virgin, Clint," she whispered, and then slithered down his body to show him that she was not inexperienced.

She nestled her face between his legs and started to lick his testicles and penis. He knew there was nothing he could do but try to keep quiet. Suddenly, her wet mouth engulfed him and her hands slid beneath his buttocks. She squeezed and sucked him at the same time, and he bit his lip to keep from moaning out loud.

"Jesus, Holly . . ." he whispered, but he had to fall silent again or cry out.

Her mouth was incredible, her teeth and tongue moving expertly on him. For just one moment he wondered where she had learned such wonderful things, and then he couldn't think anymore.

He lifted his butt off the floor and bit his lip even harder as he ejaculated forcefully. She kept her mouth on him, sucking him avidly, and he thought he was going to yell for sure. . . .

She was lying next to him, and he had almost regained his breath. Her hand moved over his chest and she kissed his neck and shoulders.

"Holly," he said, when he was able to speak again, "you have to go back to your own room."

"But we're not done," she said.

"Yes, we are."

"No," she said, sliding her hand over his belly, "we're not. . . ."

She took his semierect penis in her hand, and it immediately started to swell.

"See? We're not finished."

"Holly—"

"Shhh."

She lifted one leg over him, then climbed astride him, trapping his penis between them.

"I'll go back to my bed after I feel you inside me," she said.

"Holly, we shouldn't—"

"I'll cry out, Clint," she said. "If you turn me away, I'll wake my father."

"You little . . . that's blackmail."

"Yes," she said, smiling in the dark, "it is."

"All right, then," he said, "you'll get what you want, but my way."

She almost did cry out as he suddenly flipped her over onto her back. She spread her legs to receive him, and he rammed himself into her as hard as he could. She was wet and ready, and he slid into her so easily that his pelvis jarred into hers, making her suck in her breath to keep from crying out.

He started to drive into her, then, sliding his hands beneath her to cup her buttocks, knowing that if Buddy Bragan walked in on them now the man—his friend—would probably put a bullet in the back of his head without any hesitation.

And he'd deserve it.

"Oh . . . my . . . God . . ." she said afterward.

He had rolled off her and was lying next to her, listening intently to see if Bragan was still asleep.

"Time to go back to your own room, Holly," he said.

She rolled over and said, "I'll go, but after this you have to take me with you." She kissed him before she left and whispered urgently, "You have to!"

TWENTY-SIX

In the morning Clint decided to avoid looking in on Bragan. He was afraid he wouldn't be able to look his friend in the eye after what had happened last night. He imagined telling him:

"Last night I slept with your daughter, Bragan, but it's okay, she wasn't a virgin."

That was an understatement. The things she had done to him with her mouth and the ease with which she had seduced him attested to that fact.

No, he decided to let his friend sleep in this morning. He'd deal with Holly and her insistence that he take her with him when he left when the time came.

Outside Holly had coffee ready for them. Her father might have said something to her about it last night, because it was stronger—and better—

than it had been the night before.

"Would you like me to make you some breakfast?" she asked.

"No," Clint said, "I'll be going into the settlement early."

"What for?"

"To ask some questions."

"About who shot my father?"

"That and some other things."

They were behind the house. Her father was inside sleeping. She leaned close to him.

"About last night, Clint—"

"I don't want to talk about last night, Holly," he said. "If your father finds out—"

"He won't."

"We'll see." He handed her the empty coffee cup.

"How about a refill?" she asked.

"I'm going to saddle my horse and get going."

"Now?"

"The earlier, the better. I want to try and get some answers today."

"Wait!"

He turned and faced her. "What?"

"Who are you going to talk to?"

"Well, for one thing I'm going to talk to the sheriff," he answered.

"Mike Collins."

"Right," he said. Then he asked, "Do you know him?"

"Yes." She averted her eyes.

"Holly, how well do you know him?"

She brought her eyes back to his.

"Very well," she said, and there was no mistaking her meaning.

Clint moved closer to her and lowered his voice. "Does your father know?"

"No."

"How old is this sheriff?"

"About thirty-five, I guess."

"Aren't there any men around here your own age?" he asked.

"No," she said, "there are some *boys* around here my age, but no men."

"I see what you mean. Tell me something, how involved are you with the sheriff?"

"What do you mean?"

"I mean how's he going to act about you? Possessive? Does he think you two are in love, that you're going to be getting married? Give me some idea of your relationship."

"I'm not gonna marry him," she said firmly.

"Does he know that?"

"I suppose."

"Has he ever asked?"

"No."

"Have you ever talked about it?"

"No."

"Are there any other surprises I should know about before I go?"

"Not about me."

"About who, then?"

"Well . . . Vicky."

"What about Vicky?"

"Well, her taste in men isn't too good."

"Who are we talking about, exactly?"

"Well . . . James Wilder."

"Vicky and Wilder?"

Holly nodded.

"Is Wilder married?" Clint asked.

"Yes."

"Oh, great."

Holly frowned. "Are you attracted to Vicky?"

"Never mind that, Holly."

"You are, aren't you?"

"I have to go."

"You're not gonna take her with you instead of me, are you?"

Clint turned and said, "I thought you two were friends."

"We are, but that doesn't mean—"

"Tell your father I'll see him later."

"How late will you be back?" she called.

He kept walking and without turning around just lifted his arms and dropped them. He hoped she wouldn't follow him to the barn.

TWENTY-SEVEN

When he rode into Neverglades the place was
barely stirring. He wondered idly what the population of the place was, but as with most new
settlements, that was probably changing daily.

It was almost nine-thirty when he reined in
his horse in front of Trench's tent. Trench struck
him as the kind of man who would open early,
and close late, to take advantage of every oppor-
tunity to make money.

There was a makeshift hitching rail in front
of the place, but he ignored it and just grounded
Duke's reins. The big gelding knew enough to
stand there and wait. He hadn't had trouble with
Duke wandering off since the horse was two.

Clint went to the tent flap, found it untied,
and went inside.

"Hi."

He was greeted by a young woman with long

brown hair and a pretty, guileless face. She had brown eyes and a sweet smile, and somehow he just knew that this was going to be Jen Miller.

"Hello," he said.

"What can I do for you?"

"I was looking for Trench."

"He's not awake yet."

"Oh, I thought since the flap was untied—"

"Oh, we're open," she said hurriedly, "but he usually sleeps late."

"Who takes care of the place, then?"

"We take turns. Are you Mr. Adams?"

"That's right. You must be Jen Miller."

She made a face. "Most of the people around here call me Jen, but I prefer Jennifer, or Jenny."

"Jenny," he said. "I like it. That's my pick."

"Good," she said. "I like the way you say it."

She was wearing a simple dress, nothing daring or low-cut as most whores would have been wearing in some small western town.

"Is there something I—or one of the other girls—could do for you while you wait for Trench?"

"Uh, no, I don't think so. I'll come back and talk to him later."

"I'll let him know."

"Thanks." He turned to leave, then turned back. "How did you know who I was?"

"Buddy talked to me about you," she said. "He described you to me."

"I see."

He was about to leave when he noticed the smell of food in the air. She watched in amusement as he lifted his head to inhale it.

"You look hungry. Didn't you have breakfast?"

"No, I didn't. Is there someplace around here—"

"Come with me."

She led him to another part of the tent and he found two tables with women in various stages of dress—and undress—sitting and eating.

"Ladies," Jenny Miller said, "we have a guest for breakfast."

"Is that all he wants?" one of the women asked.

"That's all."

"Well, tell him to sit down, then."

"This is kind of you," he said to Jenny, "but I can get something to eat—"

"There's no place for you to get a good meal, Clint, believe me," Jenny said. "This is it. Come on, you can sit with me."

They walked to a table, and as they sat a heavyset woman in her fifties placed two plates of food in front of them filled with eggs, potatoes, and bacon. A basket of biscuits was already on the table.

"This is Consuela," Jenny said. "She's in charge of feeding us."

"And she does a good job too," a woman sitting across from Clint said. She was a washed-out blonde who had seen better days on the good side of forty. She was wearing a faded wrap, and her hair was tousled. She was also unself-conscious about her appearance in front of a man, which he found odd for a whore. Most of the others, even though they hadn't expected a man at breakfast, had taken some time with their appearance.

"I'm Glo," the woman said, "short for Gloria."

"Hi," he said, "Clint Adams."

"Ladies, meet Clint!" Glo shouted.

The two tables of women—seven of them all together, he counted—greeted him in unison and went back to their breakfast.

"By the time you finish eating, Trench should be awake and hungry," Jenny said. She looked at Glo and asked, "Who slept with Trench last night?"

"Milly."

Jenny turned her attention to the other table, "Milly, will Trench make it to breakfast?"

A short, rather plump woman in her thirties with brown hair and chipmunk cheeks said, "He'll be here. He didn't drink that much last night."

"You mean the lord and master was actually able to perform?" one of the other women at her table asked.

"He was randy as a rooster last night," Milly said. "I'm actually kinda sore."

"Don't think that means you're gettin' the day off," Glo shouted from Clint's table.

"I don't expect to get the day off, Glo," Milly said.

"Good," Glo said, shoving a piece of buttered biscuit into her mouth.

"The girls like to argue back and forth in the morning," Jenny said. "It's their way of waking up."

Clint looked around, then leaned closer to Jen and said, "You look like the youngest one here."

"I am," Jenny said, "although Angela claims to be."

"Which one is she?"

"The red-haired girl at the other table."

Clint leaned over to get a look. To him the girl in question looked about twenty-five.

"She likes men to think she's nineteen, but she's not and hasn't been for a while."

"How old are you?"

"Twenty," she said. "You're not gonna ask me what a nice girl like me is doin' in a place like this, are you?"

"Never," he said. "As far as I'm concerned, there's only two reasons for you to be here."

"And what are they?"

"Either you want to," he said, "or you feel you have to."

She thought about that for a moment, then nodded and said, "I expect that fits most of us here pretty well. Why are you here?"

"Here in Florida, here in this settlement, or here in this tent?"

"Take your pick."

"I came to see Buddy, and I heard he had some trouble. I'm here now to talk to Trench about it."

"About the trouble with the guns?"

"Yes."

"I hope he isn't the one."

"Do you think he is?"

"I don't know," she said. "We talk, but I really don't know him that well. I hope it isn't him, though. I like him."

"Well," Clint said, "I'm going to try to prove it isn't him."

"Just about everybody around here thinks it is," she said. "So good luck . . . you're gonna need it."

TWENTY-EIGHT

Clint was on his third cup of coffee when Trench finally walked in. The breakfast he'd eaten was just about the best food he'd had in months, and the coffee was even better. Most of the women had gone off to get ready for their day's work, with only Glo and Jenny still sitting there.

"What are you girls doin' here?" Trench asked.

"We're finishin' breakfast," Glo said.

"Looks to me like you're finished," Trench said. "Go and get ready for work."

"We're goin'," Glo said, looking at Jenny.

"Trench, Mr. Adams is here—"

"I can see he's here, Jenny," Trench said. "Get movin'."

Glo had already gone out, and Jenny now followed her.

"Consuela!" Trench shouted. "I'm ready to eat."

"*Sí, patrón,*" Consuela said and brought him a plate of food. He sat opposite Clint, in the seat Glo had just vacated.

"What can I do for you, Adams?" Trench asked.

"Bragan was shot yesterday as we were riding back to his place."

Trench stopped with a forkful of eggs halfway to his mouth. "Hurt bad?"

"He took one in the leg," Clint said. "He'll be laid up awhile."

"See who did it?"

"No."

He put the food in his mouth and frowned.

"How do you know the bullet wasn't meant for you?" Trench asked. "After all, you do have yourself a reputation."

"We don't," Clint said. "I don't think it was a coincidence, though. I mean, I don't think somebody recognized me and decided to take a shot at me."

"What, then?"

"Maybe somebody doesn't want me helping Bragan out. Somebody who doesn't want me to prove he's not selling guns to the Seminoles."

"Like who?"

"Bragan seems to think Wilder might be behind it."

"Wouldn't surprise me."

"I want to talk to Wilder today, and the sheriff, but there was somebody else Bragan thought

I should talk to, and he said you could help me find him."

"Who?"

"Some Seminole named Hard Head?"

"Mmm," Trench said, nodding with his mouth full of food. There were some scrambled eggs stuck to the stubble on his face. "Little Hard Head."

"Can you help me find him?"

"Probably."

"Will you?"

Trench stared at him. "Can I finish eating first?"

"Sure," Clint said, "go ahead. I'll have some more of this wonderful coffee."

"Consuela!" Trench shouted. "More coffee."

She came bustling over and refilled both Clint's cup and Trench's.

Trench watched her walk away. "Used to be one of my whores, but now she's too old. Good thing she can cook, though. I decided to keep her around."

"What about the sheriff?"

"Collins? What about him?"

"I want to talk to him too."

"Am I supposed to take the goddamned day off and introduce you to everybody?"

"Not to Wilder," Clint said. "I already met him."

"Well, good," Trench said. "I don't want to go anywhere near that polecat."

"Why not?"

"Well, for one thing, I don't trust a man who don't use a whore." Trench gave Clint a long look across the table that Clint ignored.

"And for another thing?"

"I just don't trust him."

"Do you know his wife?"

"No," Trench said. "How would I know his wife? I don't know any woman who ain't a whore."

"Do you know Bragan's daughter, Holly?"

"Well, okay," Trench said sheepishly, "I know *her*."

"And how about Vicky Moran?"

Trench stopped eating and stared across the table at Clint. "Don't let that one fool you."

"What do you mean?"

"Just what I said," Trench said. "Don't let her pull the wool over your eyes."

"How well do you know her?"

"Pretty well," Trench said, "considerin' she used to work for me."

That surprised Clint. "As a whore?"

Trench gave him a pitying look and said, "What else?"

TWENTY-NINE

After breakfast Trench stopped to tell Glo that she was in charge.

"I'll be back after a while," he added. "I got to be Mr. Adams's social di-rec-tor."

They went out and Clint followed Trench past some of the tents and ramshackle buildings until they reached the far end of the settlement, and then kept going.

"Where are we going?" Clint asked.

"You want to talk to Little Hard Head, don't you?"

"Well, yeah."

"He lives out here. Chances are he'll either be drunk or hung over, though."

"That's okay," Clint said.

"And you might have to pay him somethin'."

"I can do that."

"I'd charge you for my time too," Trench said,

"if I wasn't doin' this for Bragan."

Clint didn't comment. He had the feeling that if he insisted on giving Trench some money the man would find a way to justify taking it.

Finally they came within sight of what looked like a pile of old wood.

"He lives in there."

"In where?"

"There," Trench said, pointing.

"That pile of wood?"

"That's it."

"How—"

"He burrowed into there one day and that's where he sleeps."

"It doesn't fall down on him?"

"I guess not. It ain't fell down yet."

"Is he there?"

"I don't know," Trench said. "You'll have to check. While you're doin' that, I'll go back and see if the sheriff's around. Come back to my place when you're done."

"Okay."

"Good luck."

As Trench started to walk away, Clint turned and called out, "Does he speak English?"

Trench turned and, continuing to walk away backwards, said, "If you pay him enough."

THIRTY

As Clint walked up to the pile of wood he was able to see that there was an entrance of sorts—that is, if he was willing to get down on his hands and knees and crawl into it. On closer inspection, however, he found that the tunnel was too small for a man his size.

"Hello!" he called.

No answer.

He leaned over and called into the tunnel, "Hello, inside!"

"Eh?"

He wasn't sure he heard right, but then the voice came again.

"Eh?"

"Little Hard Head?"

"What?" the voice called. "Whozit?"

"I'd like to talk to you, if you'll come out."

"Whatfer?"

"Well," Clint said, "how about for money?"

He took some silver coins from his pocket and jingled them in his hand. Immediately he heard something stir inside and soon a figure was coming through the tunnel. He backed up as the man came out and stood up.

Little Hard Head stood about five foot six, which explained how he was able to make it through that tunnel. His face was black with dirt, so it was difficult to determine his age. He could have been twenty, or sixty. His braided hair looked dark, but it was so dirty there could have been gray in it and Clint would never have known.

"Are you Little Hard Head?"

The man peered at him with bloodshot eyes. "Money?"

Well, if nothing else, the Seminole knew that word in English.

Clint handed him a silver dollar.

"That all?"

"For every question you answer," Clint said, "I'll give you another one just like it. Understand?"

"I understand."

"Do you know a Seminole named Otani?"

"Otani," the man said immediately, nodding. "I know him."

"Do you know—"

"Money," Little Hard Head said, interrupting him.

"Right."

Clint handed him another dollar.

"Can you tell me where I can find him?"

"No."

"Can you—"

"Money."

"You didn't answer the question."

"I did," Little Hard Head said. "I say, no can tell you where to find him. Is answer."

Damned if he wasn't right. Clint gave him another silver dollar. Then he had a thought.

"Can *you* find him for me?"

"Yes."

This time Clint was ready and handed the Indian a dollar before he could ask for it.

"Will—" Clint started, then realized he'd better phrase his questions better or he might run out of money before he ran out of questions. "I want to find Otani and talk to him. I will pay him to talk to me, and I will pay you to find him for me and tell him so. Can you do that?"

Little Hard Head's eyes cleared and he gave Clint a hard look, like he knew what he was doing.

"I can find him," he said. "It will cost you more than a dollar."

He put his hand out, and Clint gave him a dollar.

"You find Otani and set up a meeting with him today, and I will pay you ten dollars."

"Twenty."

"Ten."

"Ten for me, ten for Otani."

"Ten for you," Clint said. "I will make my own arrangements with Otani."

The Seminole thought about it for a few moments.

"Agreed?" Clint asked, and then realized he'd made a mistake.

"Agreed," Little Hard Head said with a grin.

Clint shook his head and gave the Indian another dollar.

Clint told Little Hard Head that he could contact him through Trench, then left the Seminole walking off in the other direction and went back to the settlement.

When he entered the tent, Glo was walking by, and she stopped.

"Business?" she asked, folding her arms beneath her breasts. She had changed from the faded robe to a gauzy nightgown. Her body was so thin he could see her ribs through the gauze.

"Yes," he said, "but not your kind."

"You don't know what you're missin'."

"Where's Trench?"

She jerked a thumb over her shoulder and said, "Try his private little saloon."

"Thanks."

Clint walked to the small, cordoned off saloon area and found Trench sitting at one of the makeshift tables.

"Did you see him?" Trench asked.

"Yes," Clint said. "I thought you were going to find the sheriff for me."

Trench grinned—not a pretty sight—and said, "I know. I did."

"Already?"

Trench nodded.

"How did you do it so fast?"

"Easy," Trench said, "he walked in here half a minute after I got back."

"He's here?"

Trench nodded.

"Where?" Clint asked. "I want to talk to him as soon as possible."

"Slow down," Trench said. "He's in with Milly now."

"Milly?"

"He likes the chunky type."

"When will he be done?"

"Who knows?" Trench asked, with a shrug. "You'll just have to wait your turn. Want a beer while you wait?"

THIRTY-ONE

It was half an hour before Sheriff Mike Collins was finished with Milly—or vice versa. By that time Clint was waiting for him by the tent flap. He'd refused Trench's beer, saying he'd just wait for the sheriff.

Collins went to Trench and paid him for the time spent with Milly, then turned to leave. Clint saw that the man looked to be in his thirties, then recalled that Holly had said he was thirty-five. He was just under six feet with dark hair and a bushy mustache. He stopped short when he saw Clint standing by the flap.

"Help ya?" he asked.

"I'd like to talk to you, Sheriff."

"About what?"

"Buddy Bragan."

"Who are you?"

"A friend of his."

"Got a name, mister?"

"Adams, Clint Adams."

"Don't I know that name?"

"I don't know, do you?"

"What do you have to do with Bragan?"

"I told you, I'm a friend of his."

"So?"

"I want to talk to you about this business of selling guns to the Seminoles."

"Does he want to confess?"

"No, he doesn't want to confess."

"Tell him to come see me when he does."

"He's not going to confess anything, because he's not guilty."

"So he says. Listen, I got work to do," Collins said, and tried to get by Clint, who stood his ground.

"Yesterday somebody took a shot at Bragan."

"Kill him?"

"No, they just wounded him."

"Probably just some hothead who doesn't like Seminoles with guns."

"Sheriff, what evidence do you have that Bragan is selling guns?"

"None. If I did he'd be in jail right now, wouldn't he, Mr. Adams? Adams . . . I know that name."

"I don't know. Sheriff, why aren't you trying to find out for sure who's been selling those guns?"

"Because I know who's been selling them," Collins said. "Your friend Bragan."

"You've decided that without evidence?"

"I got a gut feeling," the man said, holding his hand to his stomach. "In this business you learn to go with your gut feeling."

"When you should be going by hard evidence?"

"Look, if you'd ever worn a badge—"

"I did, a long time ago."

"You did, huh?"

Clint nodded, but Collins wouldn't let that ruin his argument.

"Well, maybe the law was different back when you wore one, Mr. Adams . . ." The man hesitated again when he said the name, then went on. "Look, I can't help you, not when I believe—"

"Just tell me what kind of investigation you've done," Clint said.

"What investigation?" Collins asked. "I look like a Pinkerton to you?"

"Then on what grounds are you accusing Bragan?"

"I told you—" the man said, but Clint finished the sentence for him.

"Your gut."

"That's right."

"Well, Sheriff, I intend to prove your gut wrong. Do you have any problem with that?"

"As long as you don't break the law, I don't have a problem at all," Collins said. "But I'm tellin' you, friend, you're making a mistake. Bragan is guilty."

"I don't agree, Sheriff."

"That's your problem, Mr. Adams. . . . I *know* I've heard that name!"

"When you figure out where you've heard it, Sheriff," Clint said, "you let me know. Okay?"

THIRTY-TWO

When Clint left Trench's, he was disappointed
with the day's yield so far. Talking to Little Hard
Head had cost him some money, but it was only
going to be worth it if the man came through
and found Otani for him.

Talking to the sheriff had brought him nothing but frustration. The man seemed convinced
that Buddy Bragan was indeed guilty of selling
guns to the Indians. It was going to take a lot of
evidence to make him think otherwise.

Clint could only hope that a talk with James
Wilder would turn up something, or the day
might be wasted.

Trench had given him directions to James Wilder's house, and he headed there now.

The house was easily the finest structure in
what Clint had decided was a poor excuse for a
town. In fact, the house could have fit into many

of the western towns Clint had been to.

There was a fence with a gate. Clint opened the gate, closed it behind him, walked up to the front door, and knocked. He stood there waiting and wondering how Wilder had gotten these materials for his house.

Just when he thought he would have to go looking for Wilder somewhere else—maybe his saloon business—the door was opened by a handsome woman in her forties.

"Can I help you?"

"Mrs. Wilder?"

"That's right."

"I'm looking for your husband."

She stared at him for a few moments, then asked, "Are you Clint Adams?"

"Why, yes, ma'am, I am."

She hesitated another moment, thinking something over, and then said, "Mr. Adams, why don't you come inside?"

"Thank you."

He went in, moving by her and brushing her lightly in the process. She closed the door and then extended an arm to show him the way.

"In there," she said, "the living room."

"I'll follow you," he said.

She led him into a small but well-furnished living room. The furniture looked expensive and well-made, and again he wondered how Wilder had been able to get all this stuff down here.

"You have a very nice home."

"Compared to the rest of the town, you mean?"

she asked, with a hint of a smile.

"I don't think it would matter where it was, ma'am," he replied.

"Oh, please," she said, "don't call me ma'am."

"Mrs. Wilder," he asked, "is your husband home?"

"No, he's not."

He was confused. "But I thought, when you asked me in—"

"I'm sorry," she said, cutting him off, "I didn't mean to deceive you. James is not home, so I thought I would be able to talk to you."

"About what?"

"About James," she said. "Are you going to kill him?"

"Kill him—ma'am, uh, Mrs. Wilder, what would make you think that?"

"I'm sorry," she said, "but I thought . . . your reputation . . ."

"What's my reputation got to do with anything?"

"Aren't you working for Mr. Bragan?"

"No, I'm friends with Buddy Bragan, and I'm trying to help him."

"Well, I'm afraid that helping Mr. Bragan puts you at odds with my husband."

"It would seem so."

"And that means that eventually either he's going to kill you, or you're going to kill him."

"Are those the only choices?"

"Knowing my husband, yes, I would say that they are," she answered.

"Mrs. Wilder, is your husband selling guns to the Seminoles?"

"Not that I know of, Mr. Adams." She frowned. "Is that your concern? Who is selling guns to the Indians?"

"Yes, it is," he said. "Bragan is being accused of it, and I'm going to prove that he's innocent."

"And how will you do that?" she asked. "By trying to prove my husband is guilty?"

"By trying to find out who is," Clint said. "If it turns out to be your husband, I don't have any control over that."

"What would you do then?" she asked. "Kill him?"

Clint opened his mouth to reply, then closed it when a thought occurred to him. "Mrs. Wilder . . . do you *want* me to kill your husband?"

She surprised him by not answering.

"Is that what this is all about?"

He watched her closely and knew her mind was racing.

"No," she said finally. "Why would I want you to do that?"

"I don't know, ma'am," he said, "that's why I was asking."

She hesitated again, then said, "I thought I asked you not to call me ma'am."

THIRTY-THREE

From Wilder's house Clint walked to the man's business. His wife had claimed not to know where he was.

"For all I know," she had said, "he's with one of Trench's women—or that one, that Vicky."

Clint felt he had one option. Trench had already told him that Wilder didn't use his girls, and since he didn't know where Vicky Moran lived, Wilder's saloon was his only chance to find the man.

When he walked in, he saw the same bartender behind the bar. It was early, and there was no one in the place but the bartender and, at a back table, James Wilder.

"We're closed—" the bartender started to say, but he stopped when Clint walked right by him with a wave of his hand.

"Wilder."

The man looked up from his coffee.

"Adams," Wilder said. "Have a seat. Coffee?"

"No, nothing," Clint said, sitting opposite the man.

"What can I do for you this early in the day?" Wilder asked.

"I'm here about Buddy Bragan."

"What about him?"

"Somebody put a bullet in him yesterday."

"That's a shame," Wilder said. "I hope they didn't kill him."

"No, he's all right."

"Why come to me, then?"

"You seem to be the man who is most convinced that Bragan is selling guns to the Seminoles."

"That's right."

"Why is that?"

"He speaks their language."

"That's the only reason?"

"Did you know that the Seminoles speak Creek?"

"Is that right?"

"That's right," Wilder said. "They're Creeks who came south years ago, and became the Seminoles."

"Well, thanks for the history lesson, Wilder, but that doesn't answer my question."

Wilder narrowed his eyes and peered at Clint's shirtfront.

"What's wrong?" Clint asked.

"I'm just checking to see if you all of a sudden

started wearing a badge." He peered some more, then sat back and said, "Nope, I don't see a badge. Guess I don't have to answer any of your questions, do I?"

"No, I guess you don't, Wilder," Clint said.

"I'll tell you something, though," Wilder said, leaning forward.

"What?"

"Your friend is guilty and there's no way you can prove otherwise."

"Well, I'm not prepared to agree with you on that point, Wilder, but I've got something to tell you."

"What's that?"

Now it was Clint's turn to lean forward.

"If I find you had anything to do with shooting Bragan, I'll be coming after you."

Clint stood up.

"You can count on that," he said, looking down at the other man.

"I'll keep that in mind, Adams."

"You do that, Wilder."

For a moment Clint wondered if he should talk to Wilder about his wife, but then he decided against it. If she wanted him dead—as Clint suspected—let the man find out about it on his own.

THIRTY-FOUR

"You're back," Trench said, "and you don't look happy."

"I'm not," Clint said. "Let me have a beer, will you, Trench?"

"Didn't get one at Wilder's, huh?"

"He wasn't open for business yet," Clint said, then added, "besides, I didn't want to spend too much time around the man."

Trench put a beer in front of Clint and asked, "What do you mean?"

Clint sipped the beer, thinking that he hadn't had one this early in a long time.

"I think his wife wants to kill him," he said around the mug.

"What?"

"Well, I don't mean herself," he explained, "but I sure got the impression that she wouldn't have been all broken up if I killed him."

"She didn't offer you the job, did she?" Trench asked.

"No."

"He's got a lot of money, you know," Trench said. "If he was to die, then she'd get it. She could probably pay a lot—"

Clint gave him a hard look and said, "I don't hire out my gun, Trench, not for any price."

Trench put his hands up. "It was just a suggestion."

"Yeah, well, put it away and don't take it out again around me."

"Hey," the other man said, "I'm sorry."

Clint finished his beer in silence.

"Want another?"

"No," Clint said, pushing the empty mug away from him. Shaking his head, he said, mostly to himself, "How do I do it?"

"Do what?" Trench asked.

"Get myself into these situations."

"You got me."

At that moment Clint wished he could just mount Duke and keep riding until he was out of Florida. This was what he got for wanting to see new places.

There was a commotion outside, and Trench stepped out from behind the bar to see what it was. For want of something better to do, Clint followed.

When they got out to the front Clint saw three of the girls trying to push Little Hard Head out the front flap, but they weren't having much luck.

"What the hell is he doin' in here?" Trench yelled.

"I don't know," Glo said, "but we can't get him out. He's too slippery—"

"Take it easy!" Clint shouted.

All the action stopped and everybody looked at him.

Little Hard Head said something in Seminole—or Creek—and pointed at Clint, nodding.

"He's looking for me," Clint said. "Leave him alone."

"Well," Glo said, "as long as he ain't lookin' to be serviced . . ."

"Why don't you take him outside and talk to him?" Trench suggested. "He makes my girls nervous."

"Yeah, sure." He walked to the Indian and said, "Come on, let's go outside."

Little Hard Head turned and went out ahead of Clint. Outside, from this angle, Clint was able to see the puckered area on the Indian's right temple, presumably where the bullet had gone in. How had the man ever survived a wound like that?

"Have you got something for me, Little Hard Head?" Clint asked.

The Indian turned and put his hand out. "Money."

"Did you find Otani?"

"I find," the Indian said. "Money."

"Will he meet me?"

Little Hard Head nodded and held his hand out. Clint relented and gave the man five dollars.

"Ten," the Indian said.

"Where do I meet Otani?"

"Same place."

"What place?"

Little Hard Head shrugged and said, "He say you know."

"Shit," Clint said. What the hell did Otani mean by "same place"? Then he realized what the answer was. After all, they had only met once. He wanted to meet Clint back where the alligators were.

Great.

"Come on," Clint said to Little Hard Head.

"Money."

"You take me," Clint said. "I don't think I can find it on my own."

"What place?"

"Someplace where the alligators are."

Little Hard Head's eyes widened. "Everglades?"

"That's right."

"I not know—"

"I can get us part of the way," Clint said, "and then you'll have to figure out the rest of the way."

Suddenly, Little Hard Head seemed to understand. "I guide?"

"Yes," Clint said, "you guide."

"More money."

Clint decided not to argue.

"All right, more money," he said. "Let's go."

THIRTY-FIVE

Little Hard Head didn't have a horse, but that
didn't bother the Seminole. He just walked to
where they had to go, and made it look effort-
less.

Clint was able to get them to the fork in the
road where Bragan had taken him down the right
one instead of the left, but he wasn't sure he
could find the place from there.

He paused long enough to describe some of
the landmarks he could recall to Little Hard
Head, who then nodded and said, "I guide."

"Right," Clint said to himself, "for more money."

Little Hard Head took Clint to a couple of spots
that weren't right, and then suddenly an area
looked familiar to him.

"I think we got off our horses here and went to

see some alligators," he said to the Seminole.

"You want see alligator?"

"No," Clint said. "Why don't we just wait here and see if Otani shows up."

Little Hard Head shrugged. Clint was paying him, so the crazy white man could do whatever he wanted to do. If he didn't want to see the pretty alligators, that was his prerogative.

Clint dismounted, walked around the area, found the path that Bragan had taken to lead him to the alligators, and knew he had the right spot.

Now if Otani would just arrive.

Greg Fellows walked into the saloon and saw his boss sitting at a table in the back.

He stopped at the bar for a beer, which the bartender gave him even though he wasn't open yet, and then he approached the table.

"You wanted to see me, boss?"

"A half hour ago."

"I, uh, just heard that you wanted me, boss."

"Stop calling me boss," Wilder said. "Sit down."

Fellows sat.

"I've got a job for you," Wilder said. "And if you screw this one up, I'll personally feed you to the alligators."

Fellows swallowed, but remained silent. He took a sip of beer to moisten the inside of his mouth, then wiped his lips with his sleeve.

"I want Clint Adams dead," Wilder said.

"You, uh, want me to do it myself?"

"Jesus, no," Wilder said. "The man would kill you before you got within twenty feet of him. And we've seen your bushwhacking skill. I want you to take as much help as you need and get it done."

"Okay, bo—uh, okay, Mr. Wilder."

Fellows started to stand up.

"I'm not done with you," Wilder said. "Sit back down."

Fellows obeyed.

"After he's dead, I want you to dispose of the body."

"Dispose of it?" Fellows asked. "How?"

"In a way that no one will ever find him."

"How's that?"

Wilder leaned forward and said, "I want you to feed him to the alligators."

Fellows frowned but said, "Well, okay, we can do that. We'll just throw him in—"

"No, no, no," Wilder said, shaking his head. "You don't understand. I want you to feed him to the alligators . . . in pieces."

"In . . . pieces?"

Wilder nodded. "Piece by piece."

Fellows stared at Wilder, not saying anything.

"First an arm . . . then another arm . . ." Wilder said, "then a leg . . . then another—"

"Uh, Mr. Wilder, I, uh, don't know if I can do that. I just—Jesus, I can kill a man easy enough but that's *butcherin'* a man and I, uh—"

"Kill him, Fellows," Wilder said, "and find

somebody who will cut him up. Get the job done, and I don't care how many of you it takes."

"Uh, okay, bo—okay."

Fellows didn't move, just in case Wilder had something else to say to him.

"What are you waiting for?" Wilder asked.

"I just—"

"Go!"

Fellows stood up and headed for the door, hoping that James Wilder never got as mad at him as he apparently was at Clint Adams.

THIRTY-SIX

"Someone . . ." Little Hard Head said.

"What?"

The Seminole pointed and said, "Someone is coming."

Clint looked and listened, but he couldn't see or hear anything. Little Hard Head was pointing out into the water.

"Where?" Clint asked.

"Listen . . ."

"I don't hear anything," Clint said, in frustration.

"Shhh," the Indian hissed.

"I don't see—"

"They come by canoe."

"Damn," Clint said, "why didn't you say so in the first place?"

Clint stood stock-still, watched and listened. Eventually, he heard the sound of a paddle in the water. He kept watching and listening and soon they came into view. He watched in fascination as two Seminoles negotiated a canoe through the water, in which there were at least three alligators that he could see. The Indians seemed unconcerned as one alligator in particular glided over to investigate them. In fact, Clint recognized Otani and watched in amazement as the Indian slapped the alligator on the snout as it went by. He watched to see what the alligator would do, convinced that it would probably tear the canoe to shreds. Instead the creature simply reversed its course and moved away from them.

The canoe came to shore with Otani in front and another brave in the back. They both stepped out, tossed the paddles into the canoe, and then dragged it up onto firm ground. That done, they straightened up and came directly toward him.

"You'll have to translate," Clint said to Little Hard Head.

"More money," the man said.

"I know," Clint said, with a sigh.

Otani and the other brave stopped right in front of Clint. He watched as Otani looked past him at Duke and asked a question.

"He says you change your mind to sell your horse?" Little Hard Head translated.

"I figured that out," Clint said, then turned and looked at the odd Indian who lived in a woodpile. He had the feeling the man's English was a lot better than he was letting on.

"Tell him no," he said. "Tell him that's not why I'm here."

Otani listened to the translation, nodded, and then asked another question.

"He say, why you here, then?"

Clint had figured that one out too.

"Tell him I am interested in finding out who is selling guns to the Seminoles."

When Little Hard Head didn't say anything, Clint turned his head and saw the man staring at him.

"What is it?"

"You did not tell me this was about guns," the Indian said in almost perfect English.

"Well, your English improved pretty damn quick, didn't it?" Clint asked.

"I did not need it before this," the Indian said. "What do you think will happen if I ask him this question?"

"Maybe he'll answer it."

"And maybe he will kill us."

"If he's the one buying guns," Clint said. "Ask him."

"Ask him what?"

Clint took a look at Otani. The man was watching them curiously.

"First ask him if he is the one buying guns."

Little Hard Head hesitated.

"I won't let him hurt you," Clint said.

The Indian looked dubious, but he finally asked Otani a question—Clint just hoped it was the question he wanted asked.

He watched Otani's face as the question was asked, but it was like a mask, passive and expressionless. When he spoke, his face remained that way. He spoke at some length, which Clint chose to find encouraging.

"He says he is not buying guns," Little Hard Head said. "He also says that he does not approve of the Seminoles buying guns, and he will do what he can to stop it."

"That's fine," Clint said, feeling good for the first time that day. "Now ask him if he knows who is selling the guns."

Little Hard Head asked the question, but instead of Otani answering directly to the Indian, he looked at Clint and shook his head.

"That's not so good," Clint said.

"Do you want me to translate that?" Little Hard Head asked.

"No." Clint took a moment, then said, "Ask him if he would be willing to try to find out for me who it is."

Little Hard Head asked the question, and Otani answered it.

"He says he will try. He says meet him here tomorrow at this same time and he will have something to tell you."

"So soon?"

Little Hard Head translated that, and Otani replied.

"He says there is only one thing he knows for sure," the translator said.

"And what's that?"

Little Hard Head said, "That there is a white woman involved."

"What?" Clint turned his head and stared at Little Hard Head.

"A white woman," the Indian repeated.

Clint looked back at Otani, but he and the other brave were already trotting back to the canoe. They slid the boat into the water and hopped in before an alligator could come and get them. Clint watched as they paddled off, moving slowly.

"How do they do that?" he asked.

"What?"

"Move a canoe through that water without the alligators attacking them?"

The little Indian waited until Clint looked at him and then said, "Slowly, very slowly."

THIRTY-SEVEN

Little Hard Head took Clint back to the fork in the trail and from there they split. The Indian went back to his woodpile and Clint rode back to Buddy Bragan's trading post to give Bragan a report on what he'd found out.

What troubled Clint was Otani saying that a woman was involved in the selling of the guns. The first two women he thought of were Holly and Vicky, but then he remembered that Trench had a whole tent full of women. It could have been any one of them.

When he got back to Bragan's store he saw Vicky's horse in the little barn. He took the time to unsaddle and see to Duke, then walked around to the front and went in that way. He found Vicky behind the counter.

"Hello, Vicky."

"Clint," she said, smiling, "I'm glad you're back."

"Oh? Why?"

She looked taken aback for a moment by the question, then said, "Well, Holly and Buddy told me you went into town to ask some questions. I'm interested in what answers you were able to get."

"Well, I learned something interesting about you, Vicky."

"Oh? Like what?"

"Well, a couple of things, actually."

"Oh," she said, before he could go on, "Buddy told me you met Trench—and he probably told you that I was once one of his girls."

"Well . . . yeah, that's what he told me. Did, uh, Bragan know that when he hired you?"

"Sure he did," Vicky said. "You know this is not such a big place, Clint. Everybody knows that I worked for Trench at one time. It's not something I'm proud of, but at that time I needed the money pretty bad."

"What happened?"

She shrugged and said, "I got out. I got fed up and got out. That's all there was to it. I came to Buddy and he gave me a job."

Clint wondered if Bragan had ever been one of Vicky's customers at Trench's. He also wondered if there was any sense in telling Vicky what Wilder's wife had said about them.

"How is he?"

"Bellyachin'," she said. "All morning. Holly's back there with him now."

"I'll go on back."

He went around the counter, but as he started past her she put her hand on his arm.

"Does it bother you?"

"Does what bother me?"

"That I used to work for Trench?"

"No, Vicky," he said, "it doesn't bother me."

"Good," she said, "because I want us to be friends."

"We will be," he said. "We are."

She smiled and moved her hand, and he went into the back.

As he started to enter Bragan's room, he saw that Holly was next to her father, trying to get him to take some soup. There wasn't space for the three of them in the room, so he stayed in the hall.

"At last!" Bragan shouted. "Somebody who can save me."

"From what?" Clint asked. "You don't look like you need saving."

"Save me from my daughter's motherin'," the big man said.

Holly gave Clint an exasperated look and said, "He's been impossible."

"So?" Clint asked. "Is he ever anything else?"

"No," she said, standing up, "he's an ornery ol' cuss whether he's shot or not. Excuse me."

She slipped past Clint and he hoped her father didn't notice how she pressed up against him.

"Why are you giving her such a hard time?" Clint asked, moving into the room.

"It's just a damned leg wound," Bragan said. "The bullet is even still in there and it don't hurt that much."

"That bullet should come out."

"Ah," Bragan said, waving a hand, "a little lead never hurt anybody. What did you find out today?"

"Well, not much in the beginning of the day. That Little Hard Head is some character."

"Ain't he? Lives in a goddamn woodpile."

"And speaks better English than anyone suspects," Clint said.

"Does he? Damn, I didn't know that."

"Well, he does."

"Did he help you?"

"Yeah," Clint said, "he helped me meet with Otani, that Seminole brave who wanted to buy my horse."

"Wait, wait," Bragan said, "start from the beginning."

Clint told him about meeting the girls and talking to Trench, Little Hard Head, the sheriff, Mrs. Wilder, James Wilder, and finally Otani.

"You talked to Wilder's wife, huh? And she said that about Vicky?" Bragan lowered his voice at the end of the question.

"Yes, she did."

"Trench tell you she was one of his girls?"

"He did."

"Did you ask Vicky about her and Wilder?"

"I didn't."

"Why not?"

"It's not important to what I'm doing, Bragan."

"Okay, then tell me about Otani—what'd he say?"

"I have to meet him again tomorrow, same place," Clint told him. "He's says he'll have something for me by then."

"He didn't give you nothin' today?"

"One thing," Clint said. "He said that a white woman was involved in the selling of the guns."

"A woman!"

"Shhh," Clint said. He stuck his head out the door and looked to see if Holly or Vicky were around.

"A woman?" Bragan repeated, more quietly.

"That's what he said."

"What woman?"

"That he didn't say."

"Can we believe what he says?"

"I think so. He said he didn't approve of the Seminoles having guns."

"And you believed him?"

"I did," Clint said. "I was looking into his eyes when he answered."

"Jesus," Bragan said, "you're puttin' a lot of store in what one Seminole brave said."

"You're the one who suggested I go to the Indian in the first place," Clint reminded him.

"I know."

"Why'd you do that if I wasn't supposed to believe him?"

"A woman," Bragan said, shaking his head. "Did you tell that to anyone else?"

"No," Clint said. "Why?"

Bragan made a face.

"It's bad enough that people suspect me," he said, "I don't want them suspectin' Holly."

"Do you suspect Holly, Bragan?"

The man pinned Clint with a hard stare.

"If I could stand up, I'd knock you on your ass for that."

"I'm just asking."

"No, Clint, I don't suspect my own daughter, and if you do, you can just hit the trail right now and get the hell out of here."

"Take it easy. I'm not saying I suspect her, Bragan."

"What are you sayin'?"

"I'm just asking questions."

"Well, stop askin' them about Holly," the big man said menacingly. "Trench has a whole tent full of women. Maybe one of them decided to go into business for herself."

"Alone?" Clint asked. "I think she'd need a man to help her."

"You think any of those women would have trouble gettin' a man to do what they want?"

"No," Clint said, "probably not."

"Well then, go back into town tomorrow and question them. And Trench."

"You suspect Trench?" Clint asked. "I thought you were friends."

"We are," Bragan said, "but Trench would never pass up a chance to make some money."

"Well," Clint said, "I'll have to look into it tomorrow. If it's necessary after I talk to Otani."

"Are you just gonna take his word?"

"I'll take whatever he tells me to the sheriff, Bragan," Clint said. "What more can I do?"

"Come to me," Bragan said, "and you and me will take care of it. That useless excuse for a sheriff ain't gonna do nothin'."

"You can't even stand up."

Bragan gave Clint a serious look and said, "You find out tomorrow who's been sellin' guns to the Indians and I'll stand up, Clint. You can just damn betcha."

THIRTY-EIGHT

Clint spent the rest of the day watching Holly and Vicky, because they were the only two women around he could watch. If one of them slipped away from the place for any length of time, he intended to follow her, but that never happened. For a business that wasn't doing too well lately, both seemed to be able to find plenty to do to keep them busy.

As early evening came, Vicky announced that she had to get going.

"Okay, Vic," Holly said. "You go ahead."

"Thanks, Holly."

"Got someone waiting for you?" Clint asked.

Vicky gave Clint an appraising look and said, "No. What did you have in mind?"

On the spur of the moment Clint said, "Is there anyplace in Neverglades where we could get a good dinner?"

"As a matter of fact," Vicky said, "there is. Are you offering to buy me dinner?"

"I guess I am," Clint said.

"Then I accept," she said.

They both left, but not before Clint caught the hard look Holly was giving him as he went out the door.

"Tell your dad I'll see him later, Holly."

"Yeah," Holly said glumly, "sure."

He and Vicky went to the little barn where they each saddled their own horse and mounted up.

As they rode away toward town, Clint asked himself if he was doing this for business or pleasure.

Greg Fellows had talked to three of the men he usually lined up for jobs like this. One of them, Raitt, said he knew a Seminole who would do what James Wilder wanted.

"He'd love to cut up a white man and feed him to the gators," Raitt said, "and get paid for it."

"Can you get him?" Fellows asked.

"Sure."

"Today?"

"If I have to."

"You have to," Fellows said. "Do it."

"When do I tell him that he's gonna have to do it?" Raitt asked.

"As soon as we see Adams again," Fellows said.

"Tonight?" Raitt asked.

"Damn it, Raitt, I don't know if Adams is gonna come back to town tonight, or tomorrow, but we got to be ready whenever he comes. You understand? We'll take turns watchin' for him, and as soon as one of us sees him he goes and runs for the rest. Understood?"

"Yeah," Raitt said, "it's understood. Right, boys?"

The other two men, Delbert and Catlin, nodded.

"Okay, Raitt," Fellows said, "go and get your tame Indian."

"Oh, he ain't so tame," Raitt said. "Most folks think he is, but he ain't."

"Well, whatever he is," Fellows said, "go and find him. We got to get set up for this, just in case Adams does show up again today."

"I'm goin'," Raitt said.

"You got third watch, Raitt," Fellows called out, "one-hour watches."

Raitt waved that he understood.

"You boys work first and second watch out between you," Fellows told Catlin and Delbert.

"What watch do you have, Fellows?" Catlin asked.

"Three watches, Cat," Fellows said, "you, Delbert, and Raitt."

"Why not you?"

"Because," Fellows said, "I'm gonna be ready to go *every* hour. Now just go out and do what you're gettin' paid to do."

"That's another thing," Catlin said.

"What is?"

"When do we get paid?"

"We get paid," Fellows said, "when Clint Adams has been fed to the alligators."

THIRTY-NINE

The woman was waiting for Greg Fellows when he came out of the saloon.

"We have to talk."

"What the hell are you doin' talkin' to me out in the open?"

"We *have* to talk," she repeated.

He looked around quickly, then grabbed her arm and pulled her around to the side of the saloon, where no one could see them unless they were actually looking for them.

"You can't be doin' this," Fellows said to her urgently. "If Wilder finds out that I'm in business for myself—"

"You?"

"Okay," he said, "that *we're* in business, he'll kill me."

"Why are you so afraid of him?"

"I don't know why I let you talk me into this."

"How about for money?" she asked. "And ain't the money been good?"

"The money's been real good," he admitted. "What's on your mind? I got a job to do for Wilder."

"Clint Adams," she said. "Do you know him?"

"Oh, yeah," Fellows said. "In fact, that's the job I got to do."

"What is?"

"Adams."

"What about him?"

"What do you know about him?" Fellows asked.

"I know that he's tryin' to prove that Buddy Bragan isn't sellin' guns to the Indians. If he does that, his next step will be to prove who is. We can't afford that, Greg, can we?"

"No, we can't," Fellows said, "but don't worry about it."

"Why not?"

"I'm gonna take care of it," he said. "See, that's the job I gotta do for Wilder. Kill Clint Adams."

"Today?"

"As soon as he shows his face," Fellows said.

"How?"

"Forget it," he said, "you don't want to know."

"Yes," she said, "I do. In fact, I want to see it for myself."

"Ha," Fellows said, "forget that."

"Why?"

"How am I supposed to explain to the other men why you're comin' along?"

"Tell them I like the sight of blood."

"You think they're gonna—"

"Tell them it makes me horny," she added. "Tell them that they'll all get their chance at me after it's all over."

Fellows stopped short, then asked, "For free?"

"For free," she said, with a smile.

"Me too?"

"Yes, Greg," she said, touching his face, "you too."

He was still thinking about it when she said, "You better decide about it real fast."

"Why?"

"Because . . ." she said, pointing.

From where he stood he couldn't see what she could see, so he moved so that the saloon wasn't in his way. He spotted Clint Adams riding down the street with Vicky Moran.

"There's your target, Greg," she said, "Better get your men."

"The damn men," he said, "are supposed to be gettin' me."

FORTY

As Clint and Vicky dismounted, they saw a woman coming toward them. As she got closer, Clint recognized her from Trench's tent.

"Mr. Adams," she said.

When Vicky saw the woman, she smiled.

"Glo, hi."

"Vicky," Glo said, "I'm sorry you're here."

Vicky frowned. "Why?"

From within the folds of her skirt the woman produced a gun and pointed it at Clint.

"What's happening?" Vicky asked. "Glo?"

"Shut up, Vicky."

Suddenly, there were three men surrounding them, and Clint could do nothing because of the gun the woman was pointing at him. Before he knew it, his gun had been removed from his holster and there were three other weapons pointing at him and Vicky.

"The great Clint Adams, huh?" a man said.

"Just Clint, thanks," he said. "I don't use 'great' anymore."

"Shut up," the man said. "Cat, go and get the horses. We've got to get going before some more people start stirring."

"Where are we going?" Clint asked.

"You'll see."

"Glo," Vicky said again, "what are you doing?"

"Like I said, Vicky," Glo said, "I'm sorry you had to be here."

"I don't understand."

"Your friend Glo," Clint told her, "is involved in selling guns to the Indians, Vicky."

"No."

"Yes," Clint said, "and my guess is that this . . . gentleman is working with her—or maybe for her."

"I don't work *for* anybody," the man said.

"His name is Greg Fellows, Clint," Vicky said, "and he works for James Wilder."

"I work for myself."

"Are you going to kill me for Wilder, or for yourself?" Clint asked.

"It doesn't really matter," Fellows said, "but both."

"I see."

Catlin returned with four horses. The two men mounted up while Fellows and Glo covered Clint and Vicky, and then they switched off until everyone was mounted.

"Where are we headed?" Clint asked.

"A little spot I know," Fellows said. "I think you'll find it interesting."

"Thanks," Clint said, "I'm always up for something interesting."

"That's good," Fellows said, "because this will be the last interesting thing you ever see."

As it turned out, Fellows picked the same spot where Clint had now twice met the Seminole named Otani. On the way he heard the men talking about another man named Raitt and someone else he was supposed to be seeing. Apparently the one called Catlin had told the man to meet them all at this spot.

Clint was cursing himself, not only for being caught off guard by the woman, but for not having another gun stashed someplace on his person. Also, because Vicky was unfortunate enough to be with him when he was stopped.

"Okay," Fellows said, "dismount."

They all stepped down from their horses and Clint looked around.

"Now what?"

"Now we're gonna go and take a look at some alligators."

A coldness formed in the pit of Clint's stomach.

"No thanks," he said, "I've already seen them."

"Walk!"

At gunpoint Clint and Vicky were led to the

water, where the alligators were swimming around. Clint looked out and counted three of them.

"When do we do it?" Catlin asked.

"We'll wait until Raitt gets here with his Indian," Fellows said.

"Isn't this going to look a little suspicious?" Clint asked. "Two bodies found with bullets in them?"

"Two bodies won't be found, Adams," Fellows said. "By the time the gators are done with you, there won't be anything left to find."

There was a look of pure horror on Vicky's face.

"Somebody's comin'," Catlin said.

They all turned and saw a man ride up, with an Indian who was on foot.

"That's the Indian who's gonna cut Adams up?" Delbert asked.

"I know him," Catlin said. "Jesus, he lives in a woodpile, don't he?"

"I always thought he was tame," Delbert said. "What's his name . . ."

"Hard Head, or somethin' like that," Catlin said.

Now Clint understood. None of the white men would have been able to cut up his body and feed it to the alligators, so they'd had to get a Seminole who would do it. He guessed that Little Hard Head did almost anything for money.

Raitt dismounted and he and Little Hard Head

walked over to where the other men were standing.

"Here he is," Raitt said.

"Will he do it?" Fellows asked.

"He says he will," Raitt said, "for enough money."

"Will he do the woman too?"

"I guess so," Raitt said, and then repeated, "for enough money."

"Well," Fellows said, "I guess we'll find out soon enough."

He turned to Clint and pointed his gun.

"Why not let Vicky go?" Clint asked. "She's not part of this."

"She knows too much."

"Maybe," Clint said, "but she can't prove anything."

"No dice, Adams," Fellows said. "This has to be done. Boys?"

All the guns pointed at Clint and Vicky and he tensed. Was there any point in jumping them? Or jumping into the water? Wasn't that where they wanted him anyway?

He was about to do just that when suddenly Vicky screamed and started to run along the water.

"She can't get anywhere," Fellows said.

"I'll get her," Raitt said, and started after her.

He was running along the water behind her when suddenly an alligator came out of the water. Its jaws opened and snapped shut, and Raitt was screaming. . . .

FORTY-ONE

Apparently, Vicky's screaming and sudden dash for freedom had attracted the attention of the alligators. Clint couldn't believe how fast the creature had moved, and neither could the others. They all froze, and Clint took that moment to make his move.

He lunged at Fellows, grabbing the man by the shirtfront and swinging him around. Halfway around he released the man's shirt and pulled the gun from his hand. The momentum threw the man into the water, where an alligator was waiting.

Clint dropped quickly to one knee, facing the others, and hoped that an alligator wasn't coming up out of the water behind him. He fired once, and Delbert went flying from the force of the bullet.

"Son of a bitch!" the other man, Catlin, roared.

It was the sound of the shot that drew his eyes away from the alligator that was still chomping on Raitt.

He heard the shot, saw Clint, and tried to bring his gun around, but it was too late. Clint fired, and the bullet punched into Catlin's chest and knocked him to the ground.

Clint pointed his gun at Little Hard Head, who raised his hands and said, "I am not armed."

"You were going to cut me up and feed me to the alligators."

"No," the Indian said, "I would not have. I did not know it was you."

The man looked calm, even standing there with his hands in the air. There wasn't any way Clint could prove that he was lying.

"Get out of here!" he said.

Little Hard Head turned and started running.

Clint looked at Glo, who was staring out at the water where Fellows was thrashing around as an alligator dragged him out into the middle of the water.

Clint looked around quickly for the third alligator and couldn't see it.

Vicky came running back, making a wide circle around Raitt and the first alligator. This one had not dragged his prey into the water, but was working on him right on shore. Blood had sprayed for a short time, but now the man was dead and the alligator was simply chewing on a carcass.

"Clint?"

"I'm all right," he said. "That was a brave thing you did. It saved us."

"I was so scared."

"I know."

The screaming from Fellows ended abruptly, and suddenly all was quiet except for the sound of alligator jaws grinding human bones.

Clint looked at Glo, who still seemed to be in shock.

"Let's get back to town before that third alligator shows up," Clint said to Vicky. "We'll turn this woman over to the sheriff. You heard that she and Fellows were selling guns?"

"I heard."

"Also what that man Fellows said about killing me for James Wilder?"

"I heard that too."

"It won't be a problem for you to testify against Wilder?" Clint asked.

"You mean because I was involved with him? I was wondering if you had found that out. No, that was over long ago. I don't have a problem testifying against him."

"That's good," Clint said, "that's real good, Vicky." He looked at Glo and said, "Let's go."

He could take Glo in now, turn her over to the sheriff, clear Bragan of any suspicions as far as selling guns was concerned, and maybe even help him to get rid of his chief competition, James Wilder.

Then he could get the hell out of Florida.

Watch for

THE RANSOM

158th novel in the exciting GUNSMITH
series from Jove

Coming in February!

A special offer for people who enjoy reading the best Westerns published today.

WESTERNS!

NO OBLIGATION

Mail the coupon below

To start your subscription and receive 2 FREE WESTERNS, fill out the coupon below and mail it today. We'll send your first shipment which includes 2 FREE BOOKS as soon as we receive it.
